FRIEND OR FOE?

Across the railroad tracks, the tall trees sway in a breeze. They have new leaves, more gold than green. They sigh and whisper to themselves.

Mrs. Clancy has told me drug users, drunks, and perverts hang out in the woods. "You go down there by yourself, you might never come out. You'd get lost and no one would find you for years. Those woods are part of a national forest. They stretch from here to Tennessee. No telling what's hiding there."

But today I see the woods as a sanctuary.

I make my way slowly down the embankment, slipping and sliding on cinders. I look both ways. No train in sight. I run across the tracks.

Safe on the other side, I pause. Sunlight behind me, dark shade ahead of me. A branch snaps as if something stepped on it. Birds sing in hidden places. A crow caws and another answers. A breeze springs up and quivers through the leaves. Light dances from tree to tree, splashing the foliage with gold.

My skin prickles. This is a magic place, the sort of forest the Green Man might call home. I can almost feel him watching me from the trees, wondering what sort of boy I am. Will I harm the forest or be its friend?

W9-AAT-976

WHERE I BELONG

MARY DOWNING HAHN

HOUGHTON MIFFLIN HARCOURT
Boston   New York

Copyright © 2014 by Mary Downing Hahn

All rights reserved. Originally published in hardcover
in the United States by Clarion Books, an imprint of
Houghton Mifflin Harcourt Publishing Company, 2014.

For information about permission to reproduce selections
from this book, write to trade.permissions@hmhco.com or to
Permissions, Houghton Mifflin Harcourt Publishing
Company, 3 Park Avenue, 19th Floor,
New York, New York 10016.

www.hmhco.com

The text of this book is set in 12-point Chaparral.

The Library of Congress has cataloged the hardcover edition as follows:
Hahn, Mary Downing.
Where I belong / by Mary Downing Hahn.
p. cm.
Summary: "Eleven-year-old Brendan Doyle doesn't get along with
his foster mother, he's failing fifth grade, and he's bullied mercilessly
by a band of boys in his class. Then Brendan meets two potential
friends—an eccentric old man and a girl from summer school—and
he sees that there may be hope for him after all." —Provided by pub-
lisher
[1. Conduct of life—Fiction. 2. Green Man (Tale)—Fiction. 3. Foster
home care—Fiction. 4. Friendship—Fiction. 5. Bullies—Fiction. 6.
Schools—Fiction. 7. Eccentrics and eccentricities—Fiction.] I. Title.
PZ7.H1256Whe 2014
[Fic]—dc23
2013043881

ISBN: 978-0-544-23020-0 hardcover
ISBN: 978-0-544-54066-8 paperback

Manufactured in the U.S.A.
DOC 10 9 8 7 6 5 4 3 2
4500595081

For nemophilists* everywhere

Those who love the woods

We could never have loved the earth so well
if we had had no childhood in it.

George Eliot,
The Mill on the Floss

WHERE I BELONG

ONE

I'M SITTING AT MY DESK, drawing on the back of my math worksheet, not even trying to solve the problems today. What's the use? They'll all be wrong, and Mrs. Funkhauser will make some sarcastic comment about my inability to learn long division — as if I cared about something as useless as long division, which has no value in my opinion except to sort stupid kids from smart ones, and you know where that puts me. Stupid. Stupid. Stupid.

If our classroom had windows, I could watch the sky and the clouds and the trees, maybe a few birds flying past on their way to someplace where there's no math, but when my school was built they wanted something called open space. No walls between rooms. Just chest-high bookcases to divide kids up into what they call pods, which makes us all baby whales, I guess.

No windows, either—only skylights in the ceiling. You can't look outside unless you want to sprain your neck watching clouds.

Open space—how could there ever be such a thing in a school where all the spaces are closed off and you are trapped inside until you are sixteen and then maybe, just maybe, you will be free but everyone says no, you will be working in McDonald's if you don't go to college? Four more years after thirteen years of public school only with professors (what do they profess?) and majors and minors, which sounds like the army to me.

Anyway, why am I worrying about college? I'm not smart enough to go. What college would take a kid who can't even add and subtract? A kid who—

That's when I hear Mrs. Funkhauser say, "Time's up, boys and girls. Hand in your math sheets."

I look at the picture I've drawn of the Green Man. I just learned about him in a book of British myths and legends. He dwells deep in the woods and is seldom seen, partly because his face is almost hidden by clusters of oak leaves that seem to grow from his skin and sprout from his mouth. He protects the forest and all that dwell there — animals, birds, and trees. Those who respect the natural world need not fear him, but those who harm the forest will feel his wrath. Like a superhero, he fears nothing. He is just. And powerful.

My Green Man is treetop tall. He carries a sword. His beard is long and thick, his mustache curls, and his face is framed with oak leaves. His wavy hair falls to his shoulders like mine. It's the best picture I've ever drawn, and I don't want Mrs. Funkhauser to see it. I begin to slide it quietly under my notebook.

Suddenly she's beside me. "Where is your math sheet, Brendan?" The heat of her anger scorches my skin.

I don't say anything. I stare at my desk. The back of my neck feels like it's on fire.

The giggling starts. It's almost time to go home. The whales are restless. They're hoping for a last-minute Funkhauser vs. Brendan show, a high note to end the boring day.

"What's this?" Mrs. Funkhauser's eyes are eagle sharp. They see everything, even the corner of my math sheet sticking out from my notebook. With one quick move, her talons jerk my paper from its hiding place. She looks at the problems. "You haven't even tried, Brendan. What have you been doing all this time?"

I keep my head down and say nothing. *Please don't look at the back of my paper. Please don't tear up my picture.*

But of course she turns my paper over. She pauses to increase suspense. The whales squirm in their seats, ready to be entertained. Where's the popcorn? Who's got the soda?

Mrs. Funkhauser holds my drawing up for the whales to see. "Boys and girls," she says, "look at this. Brendan Doyle thinks drawing pictures is more important than math."

I *know* drawing is more important than math, but I sit there, head down, silent, waiting for the bell to ring, braced to run out the door faster than the whales. If they catch me, I'll need the magic sword I haven't got.

The whales laugh and Mrs. Funkhauser smiles at them—they're smart, they know what's important. They've learned their multiplication and long division, their fractions and ratios and decimals. They hand in their homework on time, neatly done, they follow directions, they pay attention. If they have to work at McDonald's, they will always remember to say, "Do you want fries with that?" and "Have a nice day." Their parents are proud of them. No one thinks they're weird.

Mrs. Funkhauser crumples my drawing into a small wad of paper. My heart crumples too. But I don't look up and I don't say anything. I pretend Mrs. Funkhauser is being eaten by a dragon while the Green Man looks the other way. Saving her would be a waste of time.

Mrs. Funkhauser sighs. "What am I going to do with you, Brendan?"

I shrug. I don't know what to do with me. Or her. Or anyone else.

"Why won't you do your work? How do you expect to succeed in life?"

The whales laugh. What a joke. Me succeed in life? Hah-hah.

"Get that hair out of your face. Look at me when I'm talking to you!"

When I don't move, Mrs. Funkhauser lifts my chin and forces me to look at her. "You'll never get anywhere in this world unless you change your attitude and learn to cooperate. The way you're going, you won't pass sixth grade."

As if I care. I've slid through every grade since I started school. I pass only because I read so well, not because I do my work. Besides, I hear it's bad to flunk a kid, because you'll damage his self-esteem. Maybe Mrs.

Funkhauser has figured out I have no self-esteem to damage.

"Are you listening to me? Do you want to repeat sixth grade?"

I shrug. I want to say *Yes. So I won't have to go to middle school, I can stay right here. But not in your class. In someone else's class where the teacher and all the kids will soon grow to hate me.*

The dismissal bell interrupts Mrs. Funkhauser. I leap from my seat and run. The first kid out the door, that's me. Down the steps, across the street, getting a head start. Behind me, I hear Jon Owens shout, "Run, Brenda, run!"

He and his friends chase me for maybe a block, calling me a girl, a weirdo, a long-haired freak, but they can't catch me. I'm the fastest runner in school, mainly because I've had a lot of practice eluding Jon.

From the day I walked into Mrs. Funkhauser's classroom, he and the other kids have hated me because of my hair and my attitude. Weird is what they call me. Weird is what I am. I don't belong anywhere and I don't care. I might be only twelve years old, but I know you can't trust anyone. Sooner or later, they'll desert you, betray you, turn against you, and you'll end up alone. If a foster kid learns anything after moving from house to house and school to school, it's *Don't even try to make friends.*

Even though I no longer hear Jon and his friends behind me, I don't slow down. Somehow I've ended up in the old part of town, in a bad neighborhood, on a street of big houses chopped up into apartments. Gang tags and graffiti cover street signs and stop signs, telephone poles, walls, and fences. Men linger in groups on corners. Women sit on porch steps, smoking and keeping an eye on their kids. Broken-down cars with their hoods up are parked along the street.

I definitely don't belong here, so I keep running, taking care not to look at anyone in case I offend them. Heading toward Main Street, I cut through an out-of business convenience store's parking lot. That's when I make a major mistake. I look back to make sure nobody's following me and run right into a big Harley Davidson bike parked behind the boarded-up store. It falls over with the loud noise of metal crashing onto asphalt. I fall with it, cutting my hand on broken glass. Scrambling to my feet, I see the owner of the bike running toward me, cursing.

I groan with despair. I've knocked over Sean Barnes's bike and I'm done for. Shouting a useless apology, I turn to run, but I'm not fast enough. Sean grabs a handful of my hair in his fist and jerks me to a stop. My eyes water with pain.

"I'm sorry, I'm sorry, I didn't see it, I didn't mean to," I babble in a high voice.

He doesn't let go of my hair. "You know who I am?"

My mouth is dry with fear, but I manage to nod. Everybody in East Bedford knows who Sean Barnes and his friends are. They've all been in and out of juvenile detention since they were my age, maybe even younger. They get into knife fights, they break into houses, they deal drugs in the dark corners of the McDonald's parking lot. Kids say they run a meth lab in an abandoned factory out on Muncaster Road. Everybody is scared of them, even grownups. To hear people talk, they're responsible for every crime in town.

Just last night, Mrs. Clancy, my foster so-called mother, read the local paper's crime log out loud. "Jewelry store in the mall robbed, three houses broken into, car stolen, homeless man assaulted in town park," she says, "all by person or persons unknown — Sean Barnes, in other words. He should be locked up. Not out walking the streets, stealing cars and beating up helpless old men. I won't go near that park. Even in the middle of the day, it's not safe."

And now here I am in a deserted parking lot behind a boarded-up store. Not a person in sight, and even if there were they'd look the other way. Sean has a tight grip on my hair, and two of his friends have joined him. I know their names too — Gene Cooper and T.J. Wasileski — as big and mean and scary as Sean. They're both grinning at the sight of me, their day's entertainment, the star of the show.

"What do you mean knocking my bike over, you screwed-up little punk?" Sean shoves his face close to mine and breathes cigarettes and beer in my face. His teeth are yellow. He has acne scars. And sleeve tattoos on both arms. "You need a haircut real bad," he says. "You look like a girl. But a whole lot uglier."

I try to yank free, but he holds tight to my hair. "You got a gender problem or something?"

"We can help him with that," T.J. says. "One flick of a knife and he becomes a she."

Wrapping my hair around his fist, Sean shoves me down on the asphalt so I'm face to face with the Harley. "See these scratches?" He yanks my hair hard. My nose bangs against the bike's wheel. "See where the paint's chipped? You did that, you little freak."

"I didn't mean to knock your bike over."

"Is that all you got to say?" T.J. nudges me hard with

the toe of his boot and my nose hits the wheel again. Blood drips and spatters on the asphalt.

Still gripping my hair, Sean yanks me to my feet. "Ah, look, ugly girl's nose is bleeding. And he's crying."

"You owe Sean some respect." Gene kicks my feet out from under me, and for a painful second I hang by my hair.

Sean opens his fist and lets me fall. I start to get up, but he pushes me down. "Stay on your knees and apologize."

"I'm sorry," I mutter. "I didn't see the bike. It was an accident."

"Maybe his hair was in his eyes," T.J. says. "Want I should chop it off?" He flourishes a hunting knife. The sunlight bounces off the blade like sparks of fire. I'm so scared, my insides are melting.

Sean pulls me up and shoves me toward T.J. T.J. shoves me toward Gene, Gene shoves me back to Sean. They're laughing, but each time they push me they push harder. Round and round I go between the three of them, faster and faster. I'm dizzy, I stagger, almost fall but they catch me and keep up the game.

Then, as quickly as it began, it ends. Sean lets me fall and stands there looking down at me. The sun is in my eyes and I can't see his face. He reaches into his pocket and I flinch, expecting to see a knife. He pulls out a pack of cigarettes instead and lights one, flicking the match at me.

"Girl," he sneers. "Messed-up long-haired freak. Something like this happens again, I'll give you more than a bloody nose."

The three of them get on their bikes and roar away, laughing. I scramble to my feet. The parking lot is empty, they're gone, and all that's left is my sore scalp, still burning.

TWO

I'M IN AN UNFAMILIAR PART OF TOWN, running blindly, too scared to slow down. I cut corners, dash through alleys, jump a fence, and scoot across a yard. Dogs bark at me. A horn blows and a car brakes to miss hitting me. A kid on a bike yells, "Watch where you're going!"

I finally come to a stop at the end of a road and stand there, gasping for breath, and wait for my heart to settle down. At the bottom of a hill, train tracks curve into the woods. I know where I am now. If I follow those tracks, I'll be home in less than half an hour.

I look down at myself. My shirt is stained with blood from my nose, and the knee of my jeans is ripped. Mrs. Clancy will be upset. She'll want to know what happened, who hit me and why. Soon she'll say, *Why can't you get along in school, why can't you be like other boys, if you'd just try to fit in, get that hair cut, improve your attitude, do your schoolwork, join Little League . . .*

She'll make me eat dinner and then, after I go to bed, I'll be awake all night with a bellyache. My stomach twists just thinking about it.

If only I had someplace to go besides home. A safe place where I'd belong and nobody would call me names or beat me up or laugh at me. No school. No teachers. No mean kids. No Mrs. Clancy. Just me, Brendan Doyle.

Across the railroad tracks, the tall trees sway in a breeze. They have new leaves, more gold than green. They sigh and whisper to themselves.

Mrs. Clancy has told me drug users, drunks, and perverts hang out in the woods. "You go down there by yourself, you might never come out. You'd get lost and no one would find you for years. Those woods are part of a national forest. They stretch from here to Tennessee. No telling what's hiding there."

But today I see the woods as a sanctuary.

I make my way slowly down the embankment, slipping and sliding on cinders. I look both ways. No train in sight. I run across the tracks.

Safe on the other side, I pause. Sunlight behind me,

dark shade ahead of me. A branch snaps as if something stepped on it. Birds sing in hidden places. A crow caws and another answers. A breeze springs up and quivers through the leaves. Light dances from tree to tree, splashing the foliage with gold.

My skin prickles. This is a magic place, the sort of forest the Green Man might call home. I can almost feel him watching me from the trees, wondering what sort of boy I am. Will I harm the forest or be its friend?

Taking care to move slowly, I tiptoe so as not to disturb the deep silence of the watchful trees. Here and there boulders and rocks, mossy and splotched with lichens, rise from beds of fern. Trolls taken by surprise, I think, changed to stone forever.

The trees close in behind me, and I can no longer see the light at the edge of the woods. Just shafts of sunshine lancing through the branches. It's like being in a cathedral — at least how I guess it might be. I've never been in a cathedral. Never even seen one except in pictures. But the forest has the same sort of silence and the tree trunks are tall and straight like stone columns and there's a kind of holiness here that makes you walk softly and whisper.

The snap of a twig frightens me, and I look over my shoulder. Nothing to see except leaves and shadows, but that doesn't mean nothing's there. It could be the Green Man himself, following the trespasser in his woods.

Maybe I should turn around and go home, but I didn't follow a path. There is no path. Am I lost already? I stand there, unsure what to do.

A whistle blows for the Riverside crossing, and I realize all I need to do is follow the sound of trains to find my way back.

I decide to go a little farther. Slowly, cautiously, I take a few steps, watching and listening for signs that something is following me. After a few minutes, I glimpse light through the trees. Have I come to the end of the forest already? Did Mrs. Clancy lie about its size?

I brace myself for the sight of a road and the end of the woods, but instead of utility poles and cars and stores, I find myself in a clearing. In its center is the biggest tree of all, the king of trees, rising from the earth like a huge dancing giant. Its spreading trunk forms the giant's legs, its branches thrust upward like arms.

Awestruck by its size, I touch the tree's bark, warm in the sunlight, rough against my hand. I feel its magic, its age, its power, its sap rising like blood. This tree must belong to the Green Man. Like him, it's as ancient as the earth itself.

I tip my head way back and stare up into the

branches. I long to climb all the way to the top, but the limbs are out of my reach. I walk around the trunk and discover a hollow big enough for me to walk into. Inside I see daylight far above my head. Finding a handhold here, a foothold there, I inch my way toward the sky. Wood dust and crumbling fungus tickle my nose, spider webs stick to my face, beetles scurry out of my way, but I keep climbing.

At last, I wiggle out of the hole and climb higher. I look over the tops of trees and see East Bedford pressed against the foothills. Clouds cast moving shadows on buildings and hillsides. If I raise my hand, I can block the whole town from sight. It's no bigger than a village under a Christmas tree. Tiny buildings, tiny cars, tiny people, tiny minds.

The ground is far below me, but I'm not scared. I sit on a limb and swing my feet in space. If only I could live here. I'd be happy, I know I would. And safe.

Slowly an idea comes to me. What if I build a tree house here, a secret place only I know about?

A wind stirs the leaves. For a moment I think I see a face among them. Pressing my lips against the bark, I whisper to the tree, "It's me, Brendan. Please allow me to build a house in your branches. I mean no harm."

The wind blows again. My branch sways and the leaves around me quiver. Is it a yes or a no? I'm not sure, but I think if it were a no, the wind would blow me out of the tree.

Slowly and carefully, I make my way down to the ground. It's time to face Mrs. Clancy.

THREE

Mrs. Clancy meets me at the kitchen door. "Where have you been? School let out hours ago and your dinner's sitting here getting cold."

Lit by the late-afternoon sun, her face is wrinkled and her hair is a dull reddish orange. She colors it with dye she buys at the grocery store. I'm not supposed to know that — nobody is, not even her girlfriends. But I've seen the empty boxes in the trash and I know her hair is supposed to be the color of autumn sunset.

A real mother would smile and say something like *Sit down, honey, I'll warm up your dinner.*

But foster mothers aren't real mothers. The county pays them to take care of you, so you're just part of the job. And besides, what do I know about real mothers?

Mine walked out and left me in the hospital and never came back. What did she want with a baby like me? Most likely I was weird and ugly the day I was born.

One look and off she went. She didn't leave her name or a forwarding address. Didn't tell anyone who my father was.

Once I overheard a social worker say I was a crack baby. I wish I hadn't heard that. I hope she didn't really say that, I hope it's not true, my mother didn't take drugs, she didn't, she didn't.

But maybe that's why no one adopted me. Maybe that's why I'm weird. And why I never fit in anywhere.

But what difference does any of it make? Here I am in Mrs. Clancy's house, and she's saying, "Where have you been? You should have been home over an hour ago."

When I don't answer, she takes a closer look at me. "There's blood on your shirt and your jeans are torn. Have you been in a fight?"

"No, I just tripped on something, a root or a bump in the sidewalk, I don't remember what."

Mrs. Clancy sighs. *What's wrong with this kid, why can't he behave like a sensible person, what am I going to do with him? Maybe I should send him back to Social Services.* Out loud she says, "Go clean up."

In the kitchen, she plops my dinner down in front of

me. Chicken. She knows I don't eat chicken. It was a pork chop last night, and meatloaf the night before. Growing boys need protein, she likes to say. Eating nothing but vegetables will stunt your growth and turn you into a weakling.

With a loud sigh, Mrs. Clancy sits down across from me, a cup of coffee at her elbow. She picks up a pen and studies the crossword puzzle in the evening paper. "Do you by any chance know a word that starts with an *m* and means 'messenger of the gods'?"

"Mercury," I tell her. If she read a book once in a while instead of watching TV every night, she'd know a lot more.

After I've hidden my chicken in my paper napkin — easy when she's doing a crossword — I go to my room and shut the door.

"Have you done your homework?" Mrs. Clancy calls.

"Yes," I lie as easily as I answered her question about Mercury.

"Do you want me to check it?"

"No, thanks. It was easy." Too easy to do.

"Well, I better see improved grades on your report card. You don't want to fail sixth grade."

In the living room, Alex Trebek introduces the guests on tonight's *Jeopardy!* show. Television will keep

Mrs. Clancy occupied until the eleven o'clock news is over. I open a drawing pad and begin working on a plan for the tree house.

The next day, after school and after I report to Mrs. Clancy, I run down the hill behind the house, stopping long enough to pull a rusty old wagon out of a clump of honeysuckle. I don't know who it belonged to or where it came from, but I've had my eye on it for a long time, thinking I might have a use for it someday.

Dragging it behind me, I cut down a couple of alleys and come out at a construction site. New fancy houses are going up where the skating rink and bowling alley used to be.

It's past four, and the workmen are gone. I gather up as many old boards and two-by-fours as I can manage and head for the woods. It's not stealing. Nobody wants muddy boards with nails sticking out of them.

It takes a lot of pulling and jerking, but I get the wagon across the tracks and into the woods. At first I can't find the clearing. I drag the wagon through trees and underbrush, over roots and stones, bouncing out boards and stopping to pick them up. I begin to think the forest has tricked me. I'll never see the tree again. Maybe I imagined it.

Just as I'm about to give up, I stumble into the

clearing and see it, my tree, the king of the forest, tall and broad, a dancing man, a Green Man in disguise, his face hidden.

I stare up into the tree's massive branches and search the leaves with my eyes and ears for him, but he's not there. If I listen hard enough, maybe I'll learn the language of trees and hear the Green Man's voice.

But all I hear today is the rustle of leaves and now and then the creak of a branch. I unload the wood and go back to the construction site for more. After four trips, I'm sure I have enough boards.

But before I can begin building, I need tools. I think I know where to find them.

After school the next day, I sneak into the basement and raid the late Mr. Clancy's workshop. Nails, hammers, saws, drills — all the tools I need to build my tree house.

I spot three plastic milk crates in a corner. No telling where he got them, but it's my guess he found them behind the 7-Eleven. I also discover a pile of musty old tarps he must have used for drop cloths. I can use them for a roof until I come up with something more permanent. Last of all, I help myself to a long, thick coiled-up rope — perfect for hoisting things into the tree.

Taking care not to be seen from the house, I fill

the wagon, head for the woods, unload, and go back for more. After three trips, it's time for dinner. For once I'm glad to leave the woods. I'm really hungry. And really tired.

The next day is Saturday. I wake up early, tell Mrs. Clancy a story about needing to use the computers at the library, and disappear for the day. First I rig up a simple pulley system by climbing the tree and hanging the rope over a limb. Back on earth, I tie a two-by-four to one end and pull as hard as I can on the other end. Up she goes. Slowly slowly slowly. The rope hurts my hands and breaks more than once. The two-by-fours crash down through the leaves and hit the ground hard. At last I manage to nail a framework to the tree, so high up that you wouldn't see it if you didn't know it was there.

The whole time I'm working, I feel like somebody is watching me. I stop pounding nails every few minutes and listen. I don't hear anything. I don't see anything. But still the feeling persists. What if Sean Barnes followed me that day after all? What if he and T.J. and Gene are hiding somewhere, waiting to jump me? I expect them to step out from the bushes at any moment, jeering, cussing, making threats.

My hands shake and it's hard to concentrate on

nailing down the boards. I tell myself it's my imagination. It's rabbits and squirrels I hear. Nothing more.

Then another thought creeps into my mind. Maybe my hammering has gotten the Green Man's attention. He's watching me from the dense shade and thickets below. Am I a threat to his forest? Will I harm his tree?

I clutch the hammer and stare down into the green world. Leaves stir in little gusts of wind and shadows shift their shapes, hiding whatever lurks in the tangled branches and vines. The Green Man — violent and unpredictable, like nature itself.

I whisper to him, "Green Man, are you there?"

No one answers. The shadows continue to shift and change and dance across the leaves. Something stirs in a thicket and then it's gone and so is the feeling I'm being watched.

I pick up a nail and place it carefully. *Bang bang bang* goes the hammer. It echoes through the trees. *Bang bang bang.* I hate making so much noise, but there is no quiet way to pound a nail into a piece of wood.

By dinnertime, I'm so tired I can hardly walk, my arms ache from using the pulley, and my hands are blistered from the rope. Luckily Mrs. Clancy doesn't notice the blisters, probably because her head is bent over the crossword. She looks up only to eat and to ask me for help. A five-letter word ending with *e* that means "furious." A four-letter word beginning and ending with *o* that means "grab bag." I mutter the answers and stagger off to bed. I can't keep my eyes open any longer, and my hands hurt so bad, I think I might cry.

On Sunday I take some of Mrs. Clancy's Motrin and cover my hands with thick white socks. Wincing with almost every movement, I saw and hoist and nail, saw and hoist and nail. Slowly the boards cover the platform, but it's hard work, especially considering how my arms and hands feel.

Only occasionally do I sense that I'm not alone. It can't be Sean. He would have done something by now. Torn down my tree house or yanked me out of the tree by my hair. So it's either my imagination or the Green Man. Or one of those drunks and crooks and perverts Mrs. Clancy talks about.

During the next two weeks, I finish the platform and stretch the tarp over a rough frame. Later I'll build a wooden roof and cover it with the tarpaper I found in the garage, probably left over from one of Mr. Clancy's projects. But for now, the tarp will do. Although it probably won't keep out the rain, I like the patterns of light and shadows on its surface, always moving and changing as the wind blows the leaves.

To make the tree house comfortable, I find a rug and an old broken-down lawn chair left by the curb for the trash men. I store books, drawing pads, and art supplies in a plastic tub with a tight lid. I don't think Mrs. Clancy will miss it. The milk crates from Mr. Clancy's workshop hold bottles of water, cans of soup and vegetables, and a flashlight, a can opener, candles, and matches in a glass jar. Food, water, and a ratty army blanket tucked away in another old plastic tub — I can live in my tree house a long time if I have to.

When everything is done except the roof, I prick my finger and press my blood into the tree's bark. Its sap blends with my blood and makes us one. I lean against the trunk and close my eyes. Peace and silence surround me. At last I've found the place where I belong.

A couple of days later, I stay in my tree house way past suppertime. It's bingo night, and Mrs. Clancy won't be home until after ten. I've been carving swords to protect myself from Sean and Gene and T.J. Or anyone else who threatens me. I find branches of the right size and shape, scrape away the bark, and carve a hilt and pointed blade. At first they looked like clumsy sticks, but I'm getting better. Eventually I hope to cut Celtic designs and runes into the wood.

When it's too dark to see what I'm doing, I stow my tools and climb down. Even though I know my way in the daylight, nothing looks the same at night. The trees seem taller and closer together. Boulders hide in shadows. Dampness rises from the mossy ground. Branches snap and break, leaves stir and rustle. I want to run, but I'll make too much noise, so I force myself to walk slowly.

Sure something or someone is following me, I look behind me. My chest tightens. What if it's Sean?

Finally I see a glimmer of light through the trees. Just ahead are the train tracks and the ordinary world of roads and houses and cars and stores and school. I turn my back on the woods, slide downhill, and run across the train tracks. About a mile down the line, I see the headlight of a train coming toward me. When I'm halfway up the hill on the other side, the engine roars by, hauling a long line of boxcars, hoppers, and gondolas, rattling and bouncing, sparks flying from their wheels.

When the train's gone, I look across the tracks at the woods, dark against the sky. Something moves on the edge. For a second, I think I see a man staring at me.

It might be the Green Man. I'm tempted to call out to him, but I'm afraid. What if it's not him? What if it's someone who doesn't want to be seen, one of those men Mrs. Clancy always warns me about?

So I say nothing and head up the hill for home.

At the house, the kitchen light is on. Mrs. Clancy has left a note on the kitchen counter telling me there's a chicken pot pie in the freezer. "Put it in the microwave on high for five minutes," she wrote, "and don't make a mess. I just cleaned the kitchen."

I fix myself a peanut butter sandwich without making a mess. All around me the kitchen glitters and gleams. Fluorescent light shines on white cabinets and bounces off white countertops. The stainless-steel appliances are sharp-edged and as cold as ice. Not a fingerprint, not a smudge, not a crumb. No dirty dishes except my own. It's like eating in an operating room.

I clean up and go to bed. I should do my homework, but why start now? The school year's almost over, and who cares if I flunk sixth grade. If I flunk enough times, I'll be so much bigger and older than the other kids that no one will dare to pick on me.

Not that I like elementary school. It's just that middle school will be so much worse.

So I slide under the covers and open *The Hobbit*. I've read the whole series three or four times, but it's still my favorite book. I wonder what I'd do if Gandalf showed up at my front door with a band of dwarves. I'd be like Bilbo, I guess — not really sure if I dared go on an adventure.

Tonight my mind wanders. My window is open and I hear the wind blowing. Rain is coming, traveling on the back of the wind. I can smell it. Tree toads are making a racket in the woods.

I get out of bed and go to the window. I should close it. Mrs. Clancy will be mad if rain blows in (*Look at this mess, water everywhere*). Instead I stand there and let the wind blow in my face. *Come, wind; come, rain.* I open my arms to the night and the wind and the first few drops of rain. Dark clouds scud across the sky. Branches toss.

I wish I were in my tree house, high up, close to the clouds, swaying with the wind. I imagine I hear the ancient oak's limbs creak and groan and scrape against each other. The woods below me are dark, no colors, just black and white. Everything moves and rustles and sighs. The Green Man stalks the shadows. I see him, he sees me. He holds out his hand, and I go with him into the Green Wood.

Headlights sweep across the yard, illuminating Mrs. Clancy's carefully tended shrubs, barbered and shaved until they look artificial, something you'd buy in Walmart. Blinded by the sharp glare, I close the window and jump into bed, glad my light is off.

Her key turns in the back door. She switches on the kitchen light and opens the refrigerator. Time for wine

(*One glass is all I have, it's good for the digestion*). She turns off the light (*Don't waste electricity*) and heads for the living room to drink her wine and watch the evening news. So many opinions she has, so many rules, so little love for anything except her house and her yard.

I hide my reading lamp under the covers (*You won't be satisfied until you burn the house down*) and return to Middle-earth. This time my mind stays with the story. I'm still reading when she turns off the TV and goes to her room (*A good night's sleep, that's what you need. Look at the dark circles under your eyes*).

FOUR

SCHOOL IS THE SAME, day after day after long, boring day. Mrs. Funkhauser picks on me about everything. No homework, failing tests, daydreaming, drawing, reading library books in my lap. The trouble I get into is endless.

Mrs. Funkhauser calls Mrs. Clancy and makes arrangements to see us after school (*Why can't you do what you're supposed to do? Are you stupid or just plain lazy? I am so fed up with your behavior*).

While Mrs. Funkhauser recites my failures, I daydream about the woods. It's June—two more weeks of school and I'll be free to spend every day in my tree house. In the meantime I have to survive this day, and the wrath of Mrs. Clancy.

"What do you mean he has to repeat sixth grade?" Mrs. Clancy asks in a voice loud enough to get my attention (*He's even dumber than I thought*).

I don't want to give myself away, so I grin at the floor. No middle school next year — my wish come true. No, not completely true. What I wish is to be through with school and all that goes with it forever, safe in my tree house, deep in the woods, all by myself.

"I recommend summer school," Mrs. Funkhauser says. "If he passes the tests before school starts in the fall, he can go on to seventh grade with the rest of his class."

No. My smirk vanishes, wiped clean by the threat of summer school. I won't go. They can't make me. Summer is mine. Mine.

"That's a good idea," Mrs. Clancy says, suddenly all chummy with Mrs. Funkhauser.

"What do you think, Brendan?" Mrs. Funkhauser's small brown eyes try to get inside my head, but I block them.

I shrug. "I'm not going to summer school."

"Surely you don't want to repeat sixth grade?"

"Maybe I like sixth grade," I say.

"I don't know what to do with him," Mrs. Clancy tells Mrs. Funkhauser. "I'm at my wit's end."

Wit's end, wit's end. I roll the words around in my head silently, liking the sound of them. I live at wit's end. It's a place you go when there's nowhere else to go. Mrs. Clancy knows nothing about it. Her wits were lost a long time ago.

"It's very frustrating," Mrs. Funkhauser says. "He's not stupid, you know. I've seen his test scores. He simply doesn't try. He reads, draws, and daydreams."

Now they're talking about me like I'm not sitting in the same room with them. Well, in a way I'm not. I'm down in the woods, far away from them, beyond the sound of their voices as tinny as insects talking on a telephone.

"He should be tested for ADD," Mrs. Funkhauser says.

"ADD?" Mrs. Clancy echoes.

It sounds like a fatal disease. Something exotic transmitted by evil creatures who live deep in the sewer. If I have it, I'll be dead in six months.

"Attention-deficit disorder," Mrs. Funkhauser says.

Mrs. Clancy sighs. "When I was young, you were sent to the principal if you didn't pay attention. You'd be paddled or kept after school."

"I can set up an appointment with the school psychologist," Mrs. Funkhauser says.

"Is there a charge for that?"

"No, of course not."

"I'll think about it. (*It's too much trouble, lazy brat, he's not worth it, attention-deficit disorder my foot*.) She gets to her feet, frowning. "Thank you for your time. I'll enroll him in summer school. No matter what he says, I'm sure he doesn't want to repeat sixth grade."

That shows how little she knows me and what I think, but it doesn't matter. I already have a plan for the summer and it doesn't include school.

Mrs. Funkhauser stands up too. "Thanks for coming in, Mrs. Clancy. I hope you'll reconsider the testing. I hate to see a smart boy waste his intelligence."

"He wouldn't be the first person to waste his intelligence," Mrs. Clancy says. "Kids today have no respect for anything. They don't care about school or making anything of themselves. They're looking for the easy way out. Just look at all the young girls having babies and living on welfare."

Mrs. Funkhauser looks puzzled. What do girls living on welfare have to do with attention-deficit disorder? Maybe that's how they got pregnant? They weren't paying attention?

Mrs. Clancy walks out of the classroom as if she has

something important to do. Go home, have a cup of coffee, and watch TV, that's what she has to do.

On the last day of school, Mrs. Funkhauser hands out our report cards. The other kids give each other high-fives. They're going to middle school. Hooray.

Careful to shield it from the prying eyes of the girl behind me, I take a quick look at my report. I've flunked everything except art. As predicted, I'm not going to middle school next fall — unless I do well in summer school. Which I won't, because I don't plan to go.

When the dismissal buzzer sounds, I get up to run, but Mrs. Funkhauser stops me. "Not so fast, Brendan. I want to speak to you."

"Brenda flunked," a kid shouts as he dashes out the door. "He's too dumb to leave baby school!"

Mrs. Funkhauser frowns. "Come here, Brendan."

I approach the dragon's lair, a desk piled high with grade books, textbooks, and papers. If there's any treasure, it's well hidden.

She pulls a sheet out of the pile. "This is your enrollment form for summer school. Please give it to your mother — your foster mother, that is — and have her fill it out."

I take it.

"I warned you this would happen," she says.

I nod. Does that mouth know how to smile, I wonder.

"You're a smart boy, Brendan," she says in the fake voice adults use when they're pretending to be sincerely concerned about you. "I don't understand why you refuse to do your schoolwork."

I shrug.

"You can't spend your whole life drawing and daydreaming."

Why not, I wonder.

"Look at me when I talk to you, Brendan." Her voice is the dragon's now. No more pretending. She hates me.

"Can I go now?"

She sighs. Not sadly. She's angry. "I don't think I've taught you anything this year."

She's right. I back away from the desk. "I have to go," I mumble.

"Suit yourself." She stands up, her face flushed.

Without looking back, I leave the classroom. Next year I'll have a different teacher, but Mrs. Funkhauser is sure to give a full report on me, enumerating my faults, which I don't need to repeat here, since everyone, including me, knows them already.

No need to stop at the house today. Mrs. Clancy's at work. She has a part-time job at the card shop in the mall. I watched her there once. She didn't see me. It's amazing how nice she can be to strangers. I guess that's how she talked the social worker into giving me to her (*Biggest mistake I ever made, the boy never appreciates a thing I do for him. He won't even call me Mom*).

As soon as I cross the train tracks, I leave the ordinary world behind. The trees close in around me, deep and green and thick enough to hide me. I walk silently, a warrior's walk disturbing nothing, attracting no attention, slipping from one dapple of sunshine to the next. A crow calls once, twice, three times. I stop and listen. Is it warning someone I'm here? I stand still, testing my hearing, my vision, straining to glimpse the Green Man.

The crow caws again, farther away now, making its dark way through the woods.

I climb to the platform and get my carving knife. Last week I found a fallen branch that hid a face in the twist and grain of the wood. Now I'm trying to free the face, to reveal its eyes, its nose, its mouth almost hidden by its beard and mustache. I think it's going to be the Green Man.

After a while, I notice the shadows are lengthening. The ground below me is darker than the branches over my head. Mrs. Clancy is home now, fixing dinner and fussing to herself about me (*Where is that boy, he knows it's dinnertime, if his food is cold he has no one to blame but himself*).

Reluctantly I put my knife and my carving into a hollow in the trunk and climb down. As soon as I step away from the tree, I sense someone nearby. A smell, maybe, a soundless movement, a stirring in the underbrush. I freeze and wait. Am I afraid? Maybe. Am I excited? Maybe. Should I run? If I do, will it chase me? Maybe maybe maybe.

At last, I whisper, "Who's there?" Immediately I feel stupid for asking such a silly, unoriginal question.

Of course there's no answer. Whatever I sensed is gone. Alone in the early summer twilight, I walk slowly through the woods, cross the tracks without looking back, and climb the hill toward the house.

The first thing Mrs. Clancy wants to see is my report card. I make an elaborate search of my pockets and shake my head. "I don't know what happened to it," I tell her. "It must have fallen out on the way home." Fallen into the trash can by the school steps, I think but do not say.

"Did you pass?"

"Of course I did."

She looks at me sharply (*Little liar, do you expect me to believe that?*). "I'll call the school tomorrow," she says.

After dinner, I retreat to the safety of my bed and read *The Hobbit* until I'm too tired to follow the words. Then I lie awake in the dark and think about the Green Man. Was he hiding in the shadows watching me? Surely he'll make himself known to me soon. I've treated his woods and his creatures with dignity and respect. He must see I'm worthy.

But in my head, I hear Mrs. Clancy: *Worthy? You think you're worthy? Worthy of what?*

She's never actually said this, or, for that matter, most of the things I imagine her saying. It's what she *thinks*, though.

What, you can read my mind? Don't make me laugh.

I wish I could turn off her voice. It's like a radio without a volume control. It plays on and on in my head, one terrible song after another. *You can't, you're not smart enough, you don't know what you're talking about, you're selfish and inconsiderate, and all you think about is yourself. What's going to become of you?*

I pull the pillow over my head, but it doesn't silence Mrs. Clancy. Nothing silences Mrs. Clancy.

FIVE

WHEN MRS. CLANCY comes home from work the next day, she says, "I stopped at your school this afternoon and talked to Mrs. Funkhauser. She told me she had no choice but to fail you."

She waves a copy of my report card. "While I was there, I enrolled you in summer school. You better pass so you can go on to seventh grade with your classmates."

Tossing my report card on the table, she adds, "Classes start next week at nine a.m. I'll drive you there myself."

During dinner, she goes on and on about how disappointed in me she is. "F's in everything except an A in art," she says. "Where do you think that will get you in life?"

She loves asking the big questions about *Life*. Which of course is her concept of the real world. *Life* is the place you go to die before you die. *Life* turns you into a boring person who has a job he hates. *Life* dries up your brain. *Life* makes you think money and success are important. *Life* is for grownups. I don't plan to go there. So I sit at the table slowly chewing my way through lumpy mashed potatoes and gray string beans, and cover the pork chop with my napkin when she's not looking. I've heard the *Life* spiel so often, I don't need to listen.

"Don't you have anything to say, Brendan?"

I shake my head.

"I'm talking about your *Future*. Don't you care what happens to you?"

Future—just another word for *Life*.

I shrug. What happens happens, I think. No sense worrying or planning or expecting things. One speeding dump truck can wipe you off the earth.

I pick up my plate and scrape my pork chop into the garbage can, making sure my napkin still covers it. If only I had a dog. I could sneak the pork chop to him and he'd destroy the evidence. Maybe if I make it to real life, I'll get myself a dog as a reward. A big one to protect me, maybe a German shepherd or, even better, a tame wolf.

Mrs. Clancy follows me out of the kitchen. She's relentless.

"Can't I talk any sense into your head? Won't you even listen to what I'm telling you? It's for your own good, Brendan. *Your own good.*"

Funny how for my own good is always for her own good.

I don't say anything, I don't look at her. I go to my room and shut the door and start drawing.

The next morning I'm up at six a.m. and heading for the woods before Mrs. Clancy is awake. It's Saturday. Three joggers run past me on the trail along the train tracks, red-faced, huffing, sweating, their faces all screwed up. Maybe when you're grown up, running hurts. From the looks of the men, it's certainly not fun for them.

Last night I waited until Mrs. Clancy went to bed— she was on Facebook later than usual, probably posting messages about the ungrateful, difficult, moody foster kid she's stuck with. But sometime after midnight I raided the spotless refrigerator for bread, fruit, and cheese. I now have plenty for myself and someone else if he should choose to join me.

I cross the tracks and head into the cool, damp woods. Quietly. Calmly. Breathing in the smells of moss and rotting leaves and dirt, listening to birdcalls of all sorts coming from every direction. One of the books I keep in my tree house is a copy of the *Peterson Field Guide to Birds of North America*.

I bought it for a quarter at the library's used book sale. It's an old edition, and mildew spots the yellowing pages, but birds don't change. A jay's a jay, a crow's a crow, a red-tailed hawk's a red-tailed hawk. I've learned to identify almost every bird in the woods, not only by its song but also by its appearance. I hear wrens in the thickets and mockingbirds and cardinals in the trees. A hawk cries sweetly overhead. And the crows are making a racket near my tree. Something's disturbing them, something's not right.

Taking care to make no noise, I sneak through the woods until I'm in sight of my tree. A dozen or more crows populate its branches. At first I'm puzzled. Why are they there? Why are they cawing?

Then I see him. A man is asleep on the ground under my tree. His clothes are so faded, they have no color and blend in with the earth. His skin is brown, and his beard is long and bushy. He's weathered and worn and probably as old as the forest.

I stay where I am, holding my breath. It's him. It must be. The Green Man has come at last.

But I hesitate at the edge of the clearing, still hidden in the undergrowth, just in case it's not him after all. He has a few leaves in his hair and his beard. They aren't growing from his face or sprouting from his mouth, yet I sense a sort of wildness about him. He's no ordinary man. He belongs here in the forest.

I tiptoe closer as silently as I can. I don't want to frighten him. When I'm about a foot from him, I sit down on the ground and watch him sleep. His chest rises and falls—he snores softly, sighs. Once in a while he twitches like a dog when it's dreaming.

Above my head, the crows hop back and forth on the branches and flap their wings. They caw loudly—*Wake up, wake up. There's a stranger nearby.*

The man opens his eyes. I draw back, suddenly afraid.

"Where did you come from?" His voice is deep and rumbly.

I hesitate. Does he mean literally or figuratively? I take a guess. "That's my tree house up there." I point at the platform even though it's almost invisible at this time of year.

"You live in a tree?"

I shake my head. "I wish I did."

He studies me. His eyes are kind but puzzled. Laugh lines make deep wrinkles in his cheeks. "Most boys run away when they see me," he says.

"I'm not scared," I tell him. "I know who you are."

"Is that so?"

I lean closer and whisper, "You're the Green Man. I've been waiting a long time to meet you."

He smiles and his eyes almost disappear into the network of lines surrounding them.

"This is your forest," I go on. "You protect it and all that dwell within it. Birds, rabbits, foxes, deer, squirrels. Maybe even unicorns."

"Especially unicorns," he says solemnly. "But they're rare these days. Very rare. It's been years since I've seen one."

We sit quietly for a moment. The woods are so still, I can hear the creek running over stones. A squirrel chirrs in the tree above us. The crows fly away, dark shapes in the green light of the forest. A deer bounds across a clear space near us, white tail up.

"Are you hungry?" I ask. "I brought enough food to share with you—just in case I finally met you."

He nods and I spread out Mrs. Clancy's food.

We eat together, the Green Man and I. A few

sparrows appear and peck at crumbs. The Green Man tosses a chunk of bread toward a squirrel, who wastes no time grabbing it and retreating to a branch to eat it.

"Greedy little bugger," he says. Wiping his mouth with the back of his sleeve, he turns his attention to me. "What's your name, boy?"

"Brendan Doyle," I tell him. Even though he didn't ask, I add, "I live with Mrs. Clancy. She's my foster so-called mother."

His sky blue eyes study me. "Where are your real parents?"

I tell him the truth, even though it hurts me to say it. "My mother left me at the hospital after I was born. Nobody knows who she was or where she went. Same with my father. Nobody knows who he was either."

I pause and clear my throat. I look down at the ground. I keep my voice steady. "Neither one of them wanted me. And neither did anyone else."

He starts to say something, but I clear my throat again and tell him things I've never told anyone. "So the hospital sent me to Social Services. They put me with a family specially trained to care for infants, but when I was two, they moved me to another family. I stayed with them until I was five. Then the mother had triplets, and the agency had to find a new foster parent."

What I don't tell him are the things I used to think about my mother — she had amnesia after I was born and forgot who she was, she forgot she had a baby, she might remember someday and come looking for me.

I certainly don't tell him what the social worker said, what she thought I didn't hear, that my mother used drugs and I was a crack baby.

The Green Man's voice breaks into my thoughts. "So that's when Mrs. Clancy entered the picture?"

"No," I say, "the Baileys were before her. They had a bunch of kids, some their own, others fosters like me. I didn't get along with them and I didn't try to fit in and I ran away once or twice. I didn't go far, but after the third time, they decided I was too much trouble and they didn't want me anymore."

I don't tell him the two older boys beat me up every day, that I wet my bed, that Mrs. Bailey made me wash the sheets and made sure all the other kids knew I was a baby-wet-the-bed. I didn't tell him the other foster kids told everybody at school and they made fun of me and called me names.

"So Social Services put you with Mrs. Clancy."

"Yes. I've been with her for two years."

"And what do you think of her?" The Green Man

regards me with sad eyes. "Are you happy with her? Does she treat you well?"

No one has ever asked me this. I chew my bottom lip and think about my answer. "She feeds me and all that, but she has a whole different way of seeing things and she thinks her way is the only way and I'm never going to amount to much because I don't see the same thing she sees. She's trying to make me see things her way and I don't want to so she thinks I'm stupid or something and gets mad at me. Sometimes I think she hates me."

Most people would have said something like *No, no, she doesn't hate you, she's just trying to help you,* but the Green Man doesn't say anything. He sits there watching me, waiting for me to go on.

I want him to understand what I mean, so I lean toward him and stare into his eyes. "You know how people talk about *the real world,* and *Life* with a capital *L* and all that?"

He nods as if he knows more about "all that" than I ever will.

"Well, Mrs. Clancy lives in *the real world,* but I live in a place inside my head most of the time. I draw and I read and I daydream. Stuff like school and good grades and being popular aren't important to me, but they're super important to her. I want to be an artist, pure and simple. That's all."

I pick up a stick and draw a line in the dirt. "I'm on one side of this line and Mrs. Clancy is on the other side."

The Green Man studies the line and nods. "You and I are on the same side of the line."

"I know," I whisper. "You're the spirit of the woods. You're in the *real* real world, not the fake real world."

"There are many more people on Mrs. Clancy's side of the line," he says. "You and I are a minority."

"Yes." The word comes out in a long sigh — *yessssss*.

"You spend a lot of time in the woods," the Green Man says. "I've seen you up in the tree —"

"Your tree — it's your tree, I know it is. Is it all right for me to have built a house in it?"

"It's absolutely splendid."

"I hoped you'd say that. Would you like to come up and see what it's like?"

The Green Man peers up into the leaves, his brow wrinkled with thought. "Even creatures such as I get old," he says reluctantly. "When I was a lad, I could scramble up a tree just like you, as nimble as a squirrel. But living in the wild stiffens a man's joints and slows him down."

I nod. I guess I'd been mistaken about the spirits of the wild, and I was sad to think they didn't stay young forever. "You are immortal, though."

He shakes his head. "Yes and no," he says. "When my time here ends, someone young and strong will take my place and carry on my work. So even if I die, I'm immortal. It's the work that's important, not the man who does it."

I draw my knees close to my chest and know in my heart of hearts he's telling the truth. But I wish it were not the truth.

"Tell me something, Brendan." The Green Man stares into my eyes as if he can see my thoughts swimming like fish beneath the surface. "Whenever I see you in the woods, you're alone. Do you have any friends? Someone to talk to, to share things with?"

I lower my head to hide the tears welling up. "Nobody wants to be friends with a foster kid. They hate me at school."

"That's very troubling." The Green Man sighs and tosses an apple core to the squirrel. "Very troubling indeed."

"I don't care," I say fiercely, not wanting him to feel sorry for me. "They're mean and stupid and all they care about is things you buy. And what kind of house you live in and what kind of car your parents drive. They all live on Mrs. Clancy's side of the line. Real boys, the kind who join Little League, the kind of boy Mrs. Clancy wants me to be."

"So you don't want to hit home runs and catch the ball and strike out the batter?"

"I hate Little League. Not just because I'm rotten at baseball but because Little League has all sorts of rules and everybody takes it seriously, even parents, and no one plays for fun."

The Green Man laughs. "Little League is for little minds."

I laugh too. He's the first person who has ever understood me.

"There must be a few kids who care about what you care about."

"I sure haven't met any." I'm angry now. He doesn't understand after all, he doesn't believe me. "They laugh at me and tease me and chase me and beat me up. They hate me, I tell you! And I hate them!"

I cover my mouth with my hands and wish I could take back what I just said. I've been rude to the Green Man. He must be disappointed, maybe even angry at me. At any moment, he'll get to his feet and vanish into the woods, and I'll never see him again.

"I'm sorry," I tell him. "I didn't mean to shout at you. Don't be angry."

"Why would I be angry?" He looks puzzled.

I realize I'm acting as if he's an ordinary adult who gets mad at disrespectful kids. "I don't know," I mumble. "I guess I forgot who you are."

"Sometimes I forget who I am too." He laughs, a big, jolly laugh that rolls through the trees. The kind of laugh that makes other people laugh too.

I climb the tree and come back with my drawing stuff and some of my weapons and carvings. He looks at each one carefully. He really sees my drawings. Doesn't say *Oh, this is good, you have talent* and then flip to the next one. He sighs and mumbles and takes in every detail. He turns the wooden swords and staffs over and looks at them from every angle, squinting to see if they're straight and true.

The last one I show him is the Green Man's face I carved yesterday. "It's not finished yet," I tell him, "but can you tell who it is?"

He smiles and sighs and turns the face this way and that way. "Is it me?" he asks at last.

I nod. "I found your face and beard in the grain of the wood."

"But you hadn't even seen me then."

"No, but I've glimpsed your face in the leaves and I've seen pictures in books and that made it easy."

"Easy? Work like this is never easy."

I smile. He does understand. "It was easy because the face was already there. All I had to do was let it out."

He chuckles. "All you had to do was let it out."

"Yes, sir." I sit back and feel the sun warm my back. I don't need to ask if the Green Man thinks art is a waste of time. Like me, he knows it's the most important thing in the world, in both the real world and the unreal world.

The Green Man gets to his feet and stretches. "Thanks for the breakfast, Brendan."

I jump up, suddenly anxious. "You're not leaving, are you?"

"I'm always leafing," he jokes.

I smile so he'll know I understood the joke, but it's a fake smile. "No, really, are you going somewhere?"

He waves an arm at the trees all around us. "I have a whole forest to tend to," he says.

"Can I go with you?"

"Not today, Brendan. Maybe another time."

"You'll come back?"

"Of course I will."

"When? When will I see you?"

"Maybe tomorrow, maybe next week—it all depends on how much work I need to do."

"I'll be here every day," I tell him, but he's already turning away, fading into the greenery as quietly as a deer. "Every day," I call after him.

But he's gone, and the woods are silent as if every bird and animal is quiet in honor of his passing.

I climb up to my platform and work on my carving. Now that I've met the Green Man, I have this strange feeling things might get better. I'm afraid to count on it, though. As soon as you let yourself believe something, you're bound to be disappointed.

SIX

SUMMER SCHOOL BEGINS. Mrs. Clancy drives me there to make sure I go. The classes aren't in my old elementary school but in the middle school I'm supposed to attend in the fall. The building is at least twice as big but much older. It was the high school once. I don't like the looks of the brick walls and narrow windows and steep stone steps. A kid could get lost in there.

While Mrs. Clancy watches, I climb the steps slowly and push open the heavy green door. The hall is crowded with kids, pushing and shouting. I don't know where my classroom is and I'm scared. There's too much going on, too much noise.

Trying not to be noticed, I edge along a wall of lockers until I see an exit sign. Without even thinking about what I'm doing, I escape through a back door into the summer heat. A teacher calls after me, but I run as fast as I can across the playground.

Can't catch me, I think. *I'm the gingerbread boy.*

Once the school is safely behind me, I slow down. Mrs. Clancy is at the mall by now, so I don't need to worry about her seeing me. The whales are most likely playing boring team sports or swimming at the country club pool. So I wander along a street lined with tall trees whose roots have pushed the sidewalk up here and there. Big old-fashioned houses sit back from the street on grassy lawns. Wedged in between them are bungalows and ramblers and brick apartment buildings. A power mower roars somewhere. Birds sing. A few cars pass me. It's not hot yet, just cool and damp with the smell of freshly cut grass. No one is waiting around the corner to beat me up.

I hear a train whistle and head for the railroad tracks. In a few minutes, I plunge into the cool silence of the woods. I look for the Green Man but he's not in sight. Disappointed, I climb up to my platform and survey the treetops. Green as far as I can see in all directions, rippling in the breeze. It's like being on a ship at sea.

* * *

A week after summer school starts, I come home from the woods at suppertime to find Mrs. Clancy waiting to pounce on me. She's the cat. I'm the mouse. She's big. I'm small. She's mad. I'm scared.

"Where have you been all day, Brendan?"

"At school in the morning and then hanging out with some kids in my class," I answer without hesitating. If I take too long to answer, she'll know I'm lying.

"And what did you learn today?"

If I tell her the truth — I learned a new shortcut to the woods, I patched my tree-house roof, I drew three pictures of wizards and dragons, I almost finished my unicorn head — she'll be outraged.

"Oh, just the usual," I say. "Some math stuff, state capitals, and what President Wilson did way back in the 1800s."

Her face is growing grimmer with every word. Maybe I went too far with President Wilson. Got too specific. What if he wasn't president in the 1800s? Maybe it was earlier, maybe it was later.

"Tell me what President Wilson did in the 1800s."

"He bought Louisiana from the French?" Or was it the Spanish?

"For your information," she says, "Wilson was

president during World War One. Afterward, he started the League of Nations."

I look at the floor. Who'd have guessed Mrs. Clancy knew that much about Woodrow Wilson? I should have said Calvin Coolidge. Most people don't even remember his name.

"It so happens I got a phone call from school this afternoon. The principal wanted to know why you haven't attended a single class."

Mrs. Clancy's eyes are boring a hole in the top of my head. What brains I have will leak out and make a mess on her spotless kitchen floor. "Where have you been? What have you been doing all this time? How are you ever going to amount to anything if you don't have an education?"

Although she doesn't say it out loud, she'd like to say, *You worthless boy, why do I even care what happens to you?*

The next morning Mrs. Clancy drives me to school, but this time she goes inside with me. Straight ahead is the principal's office. I feel sick. I have a history with principals, and it's not pretty. Mrs. Funkhauser sends me to the office about once a month. I'm used to Mr. Padgett, the principal at my school, but this is a different school and a different principal.

The school secretary leads us to the principal's office. Ms. Evans sits behind a well-organized desk. Framed pictures of three blond children (hers, I suppose) are the only nonbusiness things in sight. I imagine her kids are as perfect as they look.

"So you're Brendan," Ms. Evans says, her voice neutral, her face expressionless. "Please tell me why you have not attended a single class this summer."

I shrug and look at the floor, my favorite technique for avoiding questions.

She taps the desk with her long, sharp fingernails, *click-clack.* "Well?"

Mrs. Clancy squeezes my shoulder. "Answer Ms. Evans, Brendan."

"I don't know," I mutter.

Click-clack go the nails. "I hear you don't care if you fail sixth grade."

I shrug again. Mrs. Clancy gives my shoulder a little shake this time.

The principal gazes at me. "Won't it embarrass you to be older than the other kids in your class?"

I shake my head and look past her out the window.

The recycling truck is in the parking lot. The workers shout at each other and hurl stuff into the truck's maw as fast as they can. They take their job seriously. No fooling around. They're professional real-lifers.

Beside me, I sense Mrs. Clancy go tense with frustration. *Why does he act like this? Why is he so stubborn? What's wrong with him, anyway?*

"I don't have time for this, Brendan." Ms. Evans's voice is still neutral, her face still expressionless. "I expect you to be here every day for the rest of the summer. I expect you to do your homework and hand it in on time. I expect you to start seventh grade in the fall. Is that clear?"

Again a shake from Mrs. Clancy. Again a shrug from me.

"I'm sorry," Mrs. Clancy says to Ms. Evans. "I've tried to teach him manners, to be polite, to answer when spoken to . . ."

"It's all right." Ms. Evans gets to her feet. She's tall and muscular. She must work out at a gym or something.

"I'm late for work." Mrs. Clancy edges toward the door.

"Thank you for bringing Brendan to school," Ms. Evans says. "I'll take him to his classroom now."

For once I'm almost sorry to see Mrs. Clancy leave. I'm trapped. There's no escape from Ms. Evans.

With one hand on my shoulder, the principal leads me down a hall. "Try to cooperate with Mr. Hailey," she says. "He's a good teacher."

Ha. I bet he won't think I'm a good student.

She stops at room fourteen and opens the door. A man with a beard looks at us. His shaggy hair is collar length, not as long as mine but not regulation length either.

"This is Brendan Doyle," Ms. Evans says. "He's been truant the first week, but I'm sure he can make up the work he's missed."

Mr. Hailey is younger than most teachers. He's wearing cargo shorts and a T-shirt and those expensive rubber sandals they sell in L.L. Bean. He looks like a real-lifer pretending not to be. I don't trust him.

After he shows me where to sit, he and Ms. Evans step out into the hall, where I know she's telling him I have a bad attitude and he'll have to keep an eye on me but what can you expect from a foster child? *Take my word for it*, I imagine her saying. *He's headed for trouble.*

I glance around the room. Six kids look back. I don't

know any of them. Don't care to know them either—except for the girl sitting in the seat across from me. Long, dark curly hair, narrow face, pointed chin, chipped black nail polish, and a scar just under one eye. A dog bite, maybe. Some people might say it ruins her looks, but to me the scar sets her apart, makes her unique.

But it's more than the scar that interests me. Something's different about her. Nothing obvious, just something that makes me want to know her. Maybe it's her eyes, the palest green I've ever seen. Or the way she looks at me without blinking. Suddenly nervous, I duck my head and fidget with my notebook.

What am I thinking? Why would that girl like me? Nobody else does.

Mr. Hailey returns and says he's sure I'll fit right in and catch up quickly. He smiles. I don't smile back. It's always good to know what the game is before you start playing.

He tells us to open our math books, and my breakfast turns to lead in my stomach. Not my worst subject first. Mr. Hailey starts with a complicated problem, and I slip a sheet of paper out of my notebook and start drawing.

"We have art after lunch," Mr. Hailey informs me.

A boy in the back of the room snorts. "Didn't Ms.

Evans tell you Brendan is an artist and he should be ex-cused from everything else?"

"That's enough, Blake," Mr. Hailey says. Turning to me, he says, "Put the drawing away and pay attention. You're going to middle school whether you like it or not. Nobody flunks my class."

Ha, I think. *Just wait and see. I'll flunk if I want to.*

Mr. Hailey returns to the math problem. When no one except the girl next to me can solve it by the stan-dard method, he shows us a different way. If some kids still don't get it, he says, "Well, look at it this way." By the end of the hour, even someone as stupid as I am un-derstands how to solve problems that never made sense before. Not that I let on. I sit and stare out the window as if it's still a mystery to me.

The rest of the day goes like that. Different ways of doing things. No sarcasm. Some jokes. Some laughs. I find myself getting interested in what Mr. Hailey has to say about the environment and climate change. I just might survive summer school after all.

After school, the girl with the scar follows me down the street. I'm heading for the woods and I don't want company, so I walk faster. So does she. I hope she'll turn a corner or run up a sidewalk to her house, but block after block, she follows me.

At the end of the road, I stop and look at her. "What do you want? Why are you following me?"

"What makes you think I'm following you?" Her head tips to the side like a sassy bird's. "Maybe I'm going the same place you're going."

"And where's that?"

She laughs and points across the train tracks. "Over there, I guess."

I decide not to go to the woods after all, not with her. She might be interesting, but how do I know I can trust her? I scramble down the embankment. She's behind me, slipping and skidding, and finally falling.

I balance on a rail and watch her get up and slide the rest of the way down. Her shoes must be full of cinders and she's scraped an elbow. She joins me on the rail and walks ahead of me, arms spread for balance, wobbling a little but pretty steady on her feet despite her zebra-striped flip-flops. No wonder she fell on the hill.

Suddenly she turns and faces me, squinting against the sun. "How come you're in summer school?"

"I failed sixth grade," I tell her.

"You don't look stupid."

"I'm not. I just hate school. It's boring." I look at her. "Did you flunk too?"

"My old school didn't teach some of the stuff I'm supposed to know for seventh grade, so they put me in summer school to catch up."

"That stinks."

She does a little pirouette on the track and teeters precariously. "It's not bad with Mr. Hailey for a teacher. You'll like him. Everybody does."

"He's a big improvement over my sixth-grade teacher," I admit. "She was sooooo boring."

She nods as if she's known a few teachers like that. "By the way," she says, "I know your name because Mr. Hailey introduced you, but you don't know my name." She says this like she's Rumplestiltskin or something and I should guess her true name.

I shrug. What do I care what her name is? I wish she'd go away. I'm tired of her. She talks too much. Anyway, the Green Man might be waiting for me.

When I keep walking without asking the question, she says, "I'm Shea Browne. I was born in Guam, but I used to live in Texas and before that in Oklahoma and before that in Arkansas and before that in so many other places I can't even remember them all. My dad's in the army and we get transferred a lot."

Shea—what kind of name is that? Is it spelled

"Shay" like the Deacon's "wonderful one-hoss shay" in the poem? Or some other way? Names are so weird. You never know how to spell them.

Shea does another dance step on the rail and almost falls off. "Do you ever play in the woods?"

"I go there sometimes." But I don't *play* there, I add silently.

"How big is it? Could you get lost in it?"

"It's a national forest, so yeah, you could get lost. It goes all the way from Tennessee up here to Virginia."

She squints at the trees. "Magic things might live there."

I stare at her for a second, surprised. Maybe even scared. I'm not used to other people sharing my thoughts, so I shake my head and lie to her. "No, it's just ordinary. Kind of boring, actually. You know, trees, squirrels, birds. Nothing special."

"Then why do you go there?"

"I like to be alone." I stress *alone*. Maybe she'll get the idea I'm not about to be her friend or show her my secret places in the woods.

She frowns. A strand of hair hides one eye and the scar. "I hate to be alone," she says, so fiercely that I'm surprised. "Where I lived before, I had lots of friends, but people are snobby here. I thought you and me could be friends, but I guess you're just the same as everybody else."

Some people might feel bad for hurting Shea's feelings, but not me. I just want to get away from her. I'm sure the Green Man's waiting under the tree.

"Listen," I say, "I have to meet somebody. Why don't you go home?"

Shea's face turns red. "You are the rudest boy I've ever met. I'll never bother you again!"

She turns around and runs off the way we came, her curly hair bouncing. Even from the back she looks mad.

I almost call after her, but instead I dash into the woods and lose myself in the trees as fast as I can.

The Green Man isn't there after all. I climb up to my platform and stretch out on my stomach. For a few seconds, I let myself think about Shea and what she said. Does she really believe magic things live in the woods? I picture her small face and tangled curls, the scar on her cheek. Shea. What if she really wanted to be my friend? What would it be like?

Mrs. Clancy steps into my head and says, *Don't be stupid. Why would that girl like you? She'll dump you as soon as she makes other friends.*

Angry at myself, I open my sketchbook and start to draw a picture of the Green Man, but it's Shea's face that forms on the page. With a quick yank, I tear it out and crumple it into a ball. I have the Green Man. I don't need any other friends.

SEVEN

FOR THE REST OF THE WEEK, Shea ignores me. On the playground, she does her best to be part of the group of girls talking and giggling together, but they aren't interested in her, probably because she shoots her hand up every time Mr. Hailey asks a question. I know for a fact that most kids in summer school are there because they hate school. I also know they hate kids who like school even more than they hate school.

I probably hate school more than any of them, but unfortunately they don't like me either. In my case it's because I'm weird.

I spend all the time I can in the woods, but I don't see the Green Man. The weekend comes and goes without him. I worry that I've disappointed him somehow. That I'm not worthy after all.

But like I told Shea, the woods covers a lot of territory. The Green Man could be in North Carolina or maybe even Tennessee. Surely one of these days I'll come upon him napping under my tree. Or meet him unexpectedly by the stream. Or see him peering through the leaves, grinning at me.

One afternoon, I'm suddenly sure he's nearby. I can feel him watching me. I look over the edge of my platform, way down at the ground below. The bushes quiver in one place. No breeze blows, so it has to be him.

"Is that you?" I call softly.

No one answers. The bushes are still.

"Come out," I call, "I've got peanut butter sandwiches and apples."

Still no one answers. No one appears. I start to worry. What if it's Sean and his gang? What if they've found me?

"Who's there?" I shout.

The bushes rustle as if someone is trying to sneak away. I glimpse dark hair, a blue T-shirt.

"Shea Browne!" I yell. "I see you!"

Shea steps out of the bushes and into the clearing beneath the tree. She stands there looking up at me.

"That's the neatest tree house I've ever seen. Did you build it all by yourself?"

"How did you find me?"

She twists a strand of hair around her finger and grins. "I followed you after school last week. I've been here every day watching you and you never even suspected until now!"

Suddenly I hate her. "You're a nosy sneaky spy," I yell. "You had no right to follow me."

She shrugs and keeps on twirling her hair. "You don't own these woods."

I look at the bucket full of stones I keep on hand in case Sean and his gang come after me. I'm tempted to start throwing them at her, but she's just standing there as helpless as a baby squirrel or something.

"How do you get up there?" she asks, as if everything is settled between us and I'm going to invite her to join me.

"Wouldn't you like to know?"

"Yes," she says. "I would like to know."

"This is my tree house and no one comes up here except me."

She ignores me and begins circling the tree, probably looking for a ladder or handholds or some clue as to how to join me.

"Can you fly or something?" She sounds half serious.

"Maybe."

"Liar."

"Why don't you go home?"

"Why don't you?"

"You're the most irritating person I've ever met," I say.

She sticks out her tongue and laughs. "Takes one to know one."

I turn my back to her and concentrate on my unicorn carving. If I ignore her, maybe she'll get bored and leave.

"What are you doing?" she calls.

I don't answer.

"Are you making something?"

I don't answer.

"I saw you drawing in school," she says. "You're a really a good artist."

I bend my head over the piece of wood, but I'm so vexed that my hand slips and I cut myself and drop the unicorn. It tumbles down through the branches and lands almost at Shea's feet.

While I suck my thumb to stop the bleeding, I see

her pick up the unicorn. "Oh, Brendan," she says, "this is beautiful."

I frown at her. If I go down to get it, she'll see how to climb up to my tree house.

"Can I have it?" she asks.

"Of course not. It's mine. I haven't even finished it."

"After it's done, then can I have it?"

Before I can say no, the Green Man steps out of the bushes behind Shea. He's as ragged and shaggy as ever. "Of course she can have it, Brendan. You've got dozens of unicorns up there."

Shea stares at the Green Man, wide-eyed with surprise and maybe fright. Clutching my unicorn, she takes a few steps away from him. "Who are you?"

"He's my friend," I shout. "The Green Man, king of the forest and every creature in it."

"That's right, my lady." The Green Man doffs his hat and bows to Shea. "A friend to all who are true to the Green Wood."

"She's not true to the Green Wood," I yell. "She's a spy, an interloper, a thief. Make her give me my unicorn."

"I think you're being a bit harsh, Brendan," the Green Man says. "Not to mention a tad selfish."

"I just want to be his friend," Shea begins.

And I interrupt. "I don't want to be *her* friend."

"Well, this is a pretty turn of events." The Green Man laughs. "One wants to be friends, the other doesn't. It puts me in mind of a Shakespearean play. Perhaps I should act the part of Puck and bring peace to the forest."

"*A Midsummer Night's Dream*," Shea and I say at exactly the same moment. We look at each other, surprised to discover we both know the play. But that doesn't mean we should be friends. It just means we read a lot.

"Do you know how Brendan gets up there?" Shea asks the Green Man.

"Don't tell her!" I shout.

The Green Man smiles. "I can't tell you unless Brendan gives his permission."

She frowns at me. "If you tell me, I'll never tell anyone else. Cross my heart and hope to die. And I'll give the unicorn back to you. And never ask for it again."

"That sounds like a fair offer," the Green Man says.

"She can't bargain with something that doesn't belong to her."

"Please, Brendan," Shea says. "Please let me."

The Green Man looks from me to Shea and back again. "Let's turn our backs and close our eyes and wait

for Brendan to come down in secret. When we're all together on the ground, maybe he'll change his mind."

He looks up at me. "And maybe he'll bring those
sandwiches and apples down with him. I've got an empty
belly."

When I'm sure he won't let Shea cheat, I scoot back-
wards into the hollow trunk and climb down as quietly
as I can. I sit next to the Green Man and Shea sits on his
other side. I pass out the sandwiches and apples. To my
surprise, Shea hands me the unicorn.

"Maybe by the time you finish him, we'll be such
good friends that you'll give him to me."

Don't count on it, I think.

After we eat, the Green Man asks Shea questions
about herself. Does she like to read? Yes, all the time.
Does she love the woods? Yes, especially these woods because they seem so magical. Does she believe in magic?
She wants to believe but sometimes it's hard.

The Green Man nods. "It's easier to believe when
you're here in the woods."

"Yes," Shea says to him. "It's like an enchanted forest
in a fairy tale where anything can happen. Even you."

Something changes in me. Maybe I'll be her friend
after all. She looks at me and smiles as if she's guessed
what I'm thinking.

By now the shadows are long. The clearing around the tree has grown dark. A thrush calls, and another deep in the woods answers. Fireflies light up in dark places under the trees. They could be elves carrying lanterns to light their way through the forest.

The Green Man gets to his feet. "It's time for you two to go home to supper and for me to resume my rounds." He kisses Shea's hand and shakes mine. Bowing to us both, he strides away almost soundlessly and is soon out of sight and hearing.

"Is he really the spirit of the forest?" Shea whispers to me.

"What do you think?"

"He must be." She stares at the place from which the Green Man vanished. "He *must* be."

Together we follow the path out of the forest. After we cross the train tracks, she says, "Tomorrow will you show me how to climb up to your tree house?"

"Maybe." I peer into her pale green eyes. Yellow rings around the pupils remind me of a cat's eyes. "But you have to keep it a secret. Not just how to get up there but where it is."

"Why is it a secret?"

"I have enemies," I say, almost proudly. "Enemies who'd destroy my tree house if they knew how to find it."

Shea nods, impressed. "Are they supernatural?" she asks. "Demons or monsters or —?" Her voice falters as if she's not sure what else might roam the forest looking for me and my tree house.

"No." I picture Sean and Gene and T.J. skulking through the woods, smoking dope and cussing. Looking for me. I see their ugly faces, their mean eyes, their tattoos. "They're just ordinary thugs, outlaws, scum. . . ." My voice is rising, and I stop myself from saying more. I don't want Shea to think I'm afraid of them, that just thinking about them terrifies me.

Shea nods, but she still looks puzzled. "Well," she says, "thanks for not chasing me away from your tree. You wanted to, don't think I didn't know."

I kick a beer can and send it flying down the tracks. I watch it bounce three or four times before it rolls to a stop. "I'm not good at making friends." I don't look at her when I tell her this. She had a bunch of friends in Texas. She can't possibly understand.

"Yeah," she says. "I noticed." Then she laughs.

I laugh too.

"When you move as much as I do," Shea says, "you learn a lot about friends. How to get them. How to keep them until you move again."

"You'll make tons of friends when real school

starts," I tell her. "The kids in summer school, well, I don't think you're their type."

"You and me, though, we're right for each other." She stops in front of me and turns those eyes on me full force. "See, what I know about friends is, you have to pretend to like what they like and hate what they hate. But you, I don't have to pretend to like what you like because I like what you like." She starts to giggle. "I'm getting all tangled up in words, but you know what I mean. Right?"

"I guess." I kick another beer can, but it only bounces once.

Suddenly I want to get away from Shea. I need to think about what she said. Could we really be friends? I feel nervous, maybe even scared.

"Can I go to the woods with you after school tomorrow?" she asks.

"I guess so." I watch her scramble up the embankment and head for wherever she lives. Even if I'd said no, she would follow me.

When Shea's out of sight, I take a deep breath and walk along the railroad track, balancing the way she did.

The moon hangs low in the sky, close to Venus, and the sharp sweet smell of the woods fills my nose.

EIGHT

THE NEXT DAY, I show Shea how to climb to my tree house. Since she's a girl, I hope the spider webs will scare her, but she doesn't even notice them. Once she's on the platform, she looks in all directions, out over the green sea of leaves moving like waves when the wind blows.

"You can see so far." She points at a church steeple way far away and the Blue Ridge Mountains stacked like clouds along the horizon. "It's splendid!" She hugs herself and smiles so widely her face almost splits in two.

Next she looks at my carvings, and I tell her she can choose one. She picks a unicorn a little smaller than the one I haven't finished. Then she goes through my books and finds *A Wizard of Earthsea,* which she hasn't read.

While she reads, I draw. She's very quiet. I can think my own thoughts and concentrate on my picture.

After a while, she says, "Do you think he'll come today?"

I shake my head. "He patrols the whole forest," I tell her. "He only comes this way from time to time."

She nods, her face solemn, and returns to her book. A few minutes later, she asks, "Is he a wizard?"

"No. At least, I don't think so. Green Men have a special magic — they understand what animals and trees say. They know their secrets. They protect the forest. Guardians, that's what they are."

Shea nods. "Protecting things — that's better than casting spells." She pauses and smiles to herself in that secret way she has. "I talk to my cat all the time, but he never talks to me. At least not in a language I can understand."

"Do you think your cat understands you?"

"Definitely. He's very intelligent." She smiles. "He's a purebred Siamese. We show him at cat shows and he always wins. He has more medals and silver cups and ribbons than any cat in the world."

Shea leans over my shoulder to see what I've drawn. "Hey, that looks like me if I was a fairy princess or something."

I stare at the picture. She's right. "I didn't mean it to be you," I say, suddenly embarrassed. "It just came out that way."

"It's okay." Shea smiles. "I like it. Nobody ever drew me before."

She settles down with her book again, and I put some finishing touches on the picture. As an afterthought, I carefully print *Princess Shea of the Enchanted Woodland*.

When it's time to leave, I give it to her.

"Princess Shea" — she touches the lettering — "of the Enchanted Woodland." She smiles. "I didn't even have to ask for it."

We walk slowly and silently through the gathering shadows. Hidden in the bushes, things rustle and scurry around us. The evening damp rises from the earth, a good smell. The sunlight casts long beams through the trees. It's the sort of time you expect to see a unicorn peering at you from a tangle of leaves and vines.

We wait for a long freight train to rumble and bounce past, and then we cross the tracks. "Maybe the Green Man will be here tomorrow," Shea says.

"Maybe."

We wave goodbye. I go my way. She goes hers.

* * *

After dinner, I hole up in my room and actually do my math homework. Shea says it isn't fair if she does hers and I don't do mine. Plus she doesn't want to go to middle school without me. Someday I figure I'll have to tell her about Mrs. Clancy and how much Sean and his friends hate me and how weird I am and all that, but not yet. For the first time since I've come to this town, I have a friend. I don't want to lose her.

So that's how it goes for a while with Shea and me. Almost every day after summer school, we go to the tree house. She reads, and I draw. Sometimes I carve things out of wood, faces and figures and swords and staffs. And other times we just sit and talk, dangling our legs over the edge of the platform and gazing out over the forest.

Shea does most of the talking. She tells me about what it was like to live in Guam when her father was stationed there. Big brown snakes all over the place that ate all the birds. Jungles. The ocean as warm as bathwater. And heat you wouldn't believe in the summer, heat so thick with humidity, you were scared you'd drown on dry land. You could go swimming every day all year round. And you could snorkel and see the prettiest fish swimming all around you like clouds of color. Or rainbows. It was the best place she ever lived.

She also tells me her father and mother take her places every weekend. Sometimes they camp overnight in the mountains and roast marshmallows over a fire and sing songs. Or they go to Virginia Beach and stay in big hotels with rocking chairs on the front porch and walk on the boardwalk.

While Shea talks about trips to amusement parks and museums and beaches and mountains, my mind drifts to the stories I've told myself all my life, all versions of the same subject — my mother takes me with her when she leaves the hospital, she stops taking drugs, and she finds a little house for us.

Shea gives me a sharp little nudge in the side. "Here I am blabbing on and on while you just sit there and never say a word. How come you never tell me anything about your life? I don't even know where you live."

Before I know what I'm doing, I tell Shea my favorite fantasy, only I pretend it's true. I live with my mother, I say — my father died in a car crash before I was born. We don't have much money, so my mother and I can't afford weekend trips. But that's all right. On summer evenings we drive to a snow-cone place out in the country or get ice cream and read together on the couch. Sometimes we go to the movies.

I talk on and on, making up stuff I wish were true, and Shea never questions a thing I say.

"She's an artist," I add. "That's where I get my talent. To her, art is the most important thing in the world. It doesn't matter if you're poor. Doing what you love best is worth more than money."

I've told this story to myself so many times that it doesn't seem like lying.

When it's time to go home, we walk through the woods side by side. I feel bad when she says she wishes she could meet my mother. I tell her maybe someday both our families can get together and have a picnic or something.

The minute I walk into the house, Mrs. Clancy jumps all over me. It's her night to work at the mall. "You have ten minutes to eat your dinner."

After I gulp down my vegetables and dispose of my chicken, we drive to the mall and I have to go with her. She says she doesn't like me to be home alone until almost eleven p.m., but the truth is, she doesn't trust me — not since I lied about summer school. While she's practicing her be-nice-to-strangers skills at the card shop, I sit on a bench near the fountain and read *Slaughterhouse-Five*, by Kurt Vonnegut. Mr. Hailey mentioned it in class, said it was one of his favorite books, so I checked it out of the library. It's about war, but it's antiwar because of the terrible things that happen to Billy Pilgrim in Dresden. Not to mention the terrible things that happen to Dresden. I hope I never have to go to war.

Suddenly I realize it's late and the mall is getting ready to close. I can see Mrs. Clancy shutting down the cash register. Just a few shoppers linger, strolling along with big plastic bad-for-the-environment bags. Soon it will be time to go home.

I hear someone shouting. Something's going on in the jewelry store. Three guys are running toward me, shoving shoppers out of their way. They knock down an old woman. Their sweatshirt hoods hide their faces, but I recognize Sean, T.J., and Gene. T.J. runs right past me. Our eyes meet. There's no mistake about the look he gives me — death if I say anything to the cops about him. I nod and hunch over my book. I will say nothing to anyone. Even torture would not loosen my tongue.

By the time the security cops arrive, blowing whistles and shouting, Sean and his friends are gone. I hear the jewelry store man telling the cops they had a gun, they took all the money in the cash register, broke the glass in the display case, grabbed watches, necklaces, and rings. "It all happened so fast," he stammers. "I thought I was a dead man."

The real police arrive. "Did anybody see what happened?" one asks.

A few shoppers step forward, eager to answer questions. I keep my head down. I saw nothing. I heard nothing. I know nothing. Nothing at all.

Mrs. Clancy looks out the door of the card shop. "Brendan, come here."

Avoiding the police, who are still talking to witnesses, I'm glad to disappear into the store.

"What's going on?" Mrs. Clancy asks.

"Somebody robbed the jewelry store."

"Oh, good grief. Why does the mall waste good money paying security guards if they can't prevent things like this?"

I shake my head, glad she doesn't notice I'm trembling. T.J. saw me, he recognized me, one of them has a gun. They already hate me because of the motorcycle. What if they think I'll tell the cops?

"Did you see them?" Mrs. Clancy asks.

I shake my head. "I was reading."

"Reading. Give you a book, and terrorists could blow up the mall. You wouldn't know what hit you."

She pulls down the security gate and we leave by the back door. She looks around the huge, mostly empty parking lot. A few cars here and there but not a person in sight. We hurry to the car as if danger was hiding in every shadow.

NINE

S UNDAY I'M DOWN IN THE WOODS by myself, drawing a picture of the Green Man with a circle of animals, deer and rabbits and squirrels, gathered around him. I can't get the deer to look right. I've erased and redrawn them so much that I've almost made a hole in the paper.

The thing is, I can't concentrate on my drawing. The mall robbery was on the front page of this morning's paper. The cops have some suspects but not enough evidence to make any arrests. The jewelry store is offering a thousand-dollar reward. A mall spokesman assures the public that the mall is a safe place to shop. Security has been doubled.

Mall security won't help me if Sean decides to make

sure I don't inform the cops. What if they find me here in the woods? If Shea could follow me, they could follow me.

Every noise, every bird call startles me. I peer down from my tree house and look for intruders, study the underbrush, watch for movement among the trees. I think about the gun. My collection of weapons — wooden swords and buckets of stones — is pathetic. I have no way to defend myself against those three, even if I leave the gun out of the equation. If they come after me, I'm done for.

I hear a branch snap. A flock of crows rises from a nearby tree, cawing as if to warn me of danger. Shaking with fear, I lie flat on my belly and look down. The bushes part, and the Green Man steps into the clearing and smiles up at me. His faded clothes blend in with the dappled shadows of the trees. He's almost invisible.

"Hello, young Brendan," he calls.

Relief surges through me. I climb down, bringing a bag of sandwiches with me. I want to hug him but I'm not sure he'd like that. Instead I tell him how glad I am to see him.

"Is something bothering you?" He's looking at me closely, his eyes probing mine. "You seem nervous, upset."

Swearing him to secrecy, I tell him about the motorcycle and Sean and T.J. and Gene. I tell him how they treated me, I tell him about the mall and seeing T.J. and how scared I am that they'll get me. Once I've started talking, I can't stop. When I've told him everything, my mouth is dry and my knees feel weak, but I have a strange feeling of a burden lifting. I've told my secret to the one person I trust the most, even more than I trust Shea.

He sits beside me quietly and listens, one big hand on my shoulder. He says nothing right away, but I can tell he's thinking about what I've said.

"This Sean," he says slowly. "Is he a redhead, sharp-featured, tattoos on his arms?"

I nod. "Do you know him?"

"I know who he is," he says. "His friends, too. They're a bad lot, Brendan. Whatever you do, stay away from them."

The Green Man sounds worried, and I assure him I have no intention of going near them. "Have you seen them here, in the woods?"

"I came upon them shooting squirrels for fun and accosted them. I told them a decent person respects the lives of animals and doesn't hurt or kill them for sport." He sighs and strokes his beard, something he does when he's thinking.

"What happened?"

"Unfortunately I angered them," he says. "They called me a stupid old man. Sean pointed his gun at me and said maybe he should shoot me instead of squirrels. They all laughed. Then one of them shoved me hard enough to knock me down. They told me to mind my own business — it wasn't against the law to shoot tree rats."

"I can't believe anyone would treat you that way. Don't they know who you are?"

"Apparently not." The Green Man gives me a sad smile. "Louts like them always pick on those they perceive as weak and unable to defend themselves."

It scares me to think that Sean, T.J., and Gene could treat the Green Man as if he were just another weak old man like the sad homeless men in the park. "Why didn't you tell them who you are and smite them with lightning?"

"Believe me, Brendan, I would have liked to do that very much, but the laws of the Green Wood prevent me from meeting violence with violence. I go in peace in the forest and leave punishment to a higher authority."

I try to understand, but I wish the Green Man were allowed to punish Sean and his gang of miscreants.

The Green Man leans over and gives me a gentle

nudge. "Now to speak of more mundane matters, my belly is hoping you've brought food with you."

I pull a lunch out of my backpack and solemnly divide it between us. He wolfs his sandwich down so fast, I give him half of mine.

After he's eaten, he lies back on the mossy ground and sighs in contentment. "Nothing like a full belly."

He looks as if he's about to drift into one of his long naps, but instead he props himself up on one elbow and stares into the bushes as if he's looking for someone. "Where is my little princess of the woodland?"

"She's never here on weekends," I tell him, trying to keep the envy out of my voice. "Her parents take her places — the beach, the mountains, all sorts of places I've never been." I pick up a stick and scratch lines in the dirt. Maybe I'll draw a house. Or no — a castle might be better. With a moat and high walls and a dungeon where they keep the dragon.

"Last Saturday, they went to Kings Dominion." I concentrate on my castle while I tell him. "Shea rode the Rebel Yell five times. Today she's going white-water rafting on the Shenandoah River, near Harpers Ferry."

"I suppose you'd like to do that."

I shrug. "I might be scared."

"I wouldn't care for it," the Green Man says. "An inner tube is safer. You float along slowly. Just you and the river and the birds singing in the woods."

"Shea says the river has rapids. And waterfalls. People drown sometimes."

He frowns. "I hope she's careful."

"Me too." I picture Shea spinning down a river, heading straight for a huge waterfall. I see myself rescuing her. Perhaps I'd swing down on a rope from a tree and snatch her from the very brink of destruction. I'd be her hero.

In the back of my mind, Mrs. Clancy says, *The very idea — a boy like you rescuing someone? Don't make me laugh. You're the one who needs rescuing.*

I swat a mosquito. Where did that come from? I don't need rescuing. Or do I? *Do I?*

Suddenly the woods seem to gather around me. The air is heavy, hot and thick with humidity. Mosquitoes swarm around my head. Gnats nibble at my ears.

Nothing bothers the Green Man. He's fallen asleep and begun to snore, probably exhausted from his journey. His chest rises and falls under his old shirt. His beard is littered with cookie crumbs. I wonder how old he is. Hundreds of years, maybe. Thousands, even. He's been guarding the woods since the age of druids and knights.

I lean back against a tree. The leaves move and rustle high over my head, hiding the sky. The sun splashes down through the spaces that open and shut every time the breeze shifts. My eyelids grow heavy. It's easier to sleep than to stay awake.

When I wake up, the Green Man is gone and the shadows are long. They creep across the ground toward me. The sun's rays are parallel with the ground. It's dinnertime. I pack up my drawing supplies and head back to the other world, real to some but not to me.

TEN

———

THE NEXT WEEK, Shea and I take some boards from a construction site and drag them into the woods. I rig up the pulley and Shea helps me get the boards into the tree. With her help, the work goes faster, but it takes two or three days of hoisting and hammering to build a platform for Shea just below mine. She decorates it with a mirror she found in somebody's trash, a plastic tub with a tight lid, and a slightly crooked beach chair found by the side of the road. We take a few more milk crates from the convenience store so Shea can have her own place to keep stuff.

While we're arranging Shea's things, a familiar voice calls hello. I look down, and there he is, the Green Man himself, grinning up at us. "My word," he says, "you've built an addition just for my lady!"

Shea and I scramble down from the tree, skinning our elbows and knees and sending the spiders scurrying.

"Is it okay—do you approve?" I ask, suddenly fearful he might object to more nails being driven into his tree.

"It's lovely," he says. "Lady Shea needs some space of her own."

I want to hug him, but I hang back and watch Shea fling her arms around him and almost knock him down. "We missed you!" she cries.

"Whoa," he laughs. "Have pity on an old man." He looks at me. "Any food, Master Doyle?"

"I didn't know you'd be here," I say. "Shea and I were going to walk to the convenience store and buy lunch."

"Ah, that's fine, then."

The three us walk through the woods and follow the train tracks to Route 22. There's a 7-Eleven a block down the road. An old, dingy one. Not the kind people from town use. A beat-up dump truck sits in the parking lot. Its owner is inside buying cigarettes and a six-pack of beer. As he walks out the door, I see the Green Man's hand dart out as swift and smooth as a snake and lift a bottle from the six-pack. It disappears into his pocket without one jiggle or clink.

The dump truck driver doesn't notice, and neither does Shea. She's already in the candy aisle looking for Kit Kats, her favorite. The Green Man strolls around the store, looking innocent. He doesn't know I saw.

I turn it over and over in my mind. The Green Man stole a bottle of beer. Why did he do it? He lives in the Green Wood. There's nothing to buy there. Maybe he doesn't understand how things are done outside the woods. After all, this isn't his reality. Money doesn't exist in his world.

I take a deep breath. It's okay. I won't worry about it. The Green Man is not a thief. He can't be. His laws are different from ours, that's all.

I show him the sandwiches in the refrigerated case. He picks ham and cheese. Shea chooses tuna salad. I take egg salad. Since Shea gets an allowance, she pays for the sandwiches, three cans of soda, and a big Kit Kat chocolate bar.

The skinny guy at the cash register has been watching all of us since we came in. Maybe he saw the Green Man pocket the beer. He takes Shea's money, but he doesn't speak to us. Not even a "Thank you" or a "Have a nice day."

I look back as we leave. He's still watching us, his eyes narrow in his long, pale face.

We trudge along the tracks, crunching cinders with every step. Shea hops on the rail and walks ahead like she's dancing on a tightrope. The neck of the beer bottle sticks out of the Green Man's pocket. I turn my eyes away. No matter what I tell myself, the sight of it disturbs me.

"What's it like to live in the woods?" I ask.

"Cold in the winter, hot in the summer," he says. "But better than being cooped up inside."

He follows the path into the woods. His back is broad, his shoulders wide but rounded, kind of slumped as if he's tired. I hurry to catch up with him, to walk by his side. Shea is still ahead, darting through the woods like a bird that can't fly.

"Where were you while you were gone?" I ask. "Did you follow the Appalachian Trail down through North Carolina and into Georgia?"

"Oh, yes," he says softly. "It was a good journey."

I keep quiet, hoping he'll tell me what he's done and what he's seen, but he says no more until we're sitting under the tree, eating our lunch.

He leans back against the tree and wipes his mouth

with the back of his hand. Then he unscrews the top of his beer bottle and begins to drink.

Shea stares at him. "Where did you get that?"

"The beer?" The Green Man holds the bottle up to the light and squints at it as if he has no idea where it came from. "I believe the gentleman in the store gave it to me. Or would have if he'd thought of it." He winks at us. "Sometimes generosity must be prompted."

"You stole it?" Shea stares at him, shocked.

"*Stole* — that's a mighty strong word." The Green Man finishes the beer and wipes his mouth again. "A fellow like him can spare one miserable bottle of beer."

With that, he lies on his back and shuts his eyes. "Naptime," he murmurs.

Shea and I watch him drift off to sleep. Soon he's snoring.

"No matter what he says, he *stole* that beer," Shea whispers.

I shrug and swat at the gnats circling my head, tiny buzzing things that bite my ears and my scalp and get in my eyes. "His world has different rules," I say. "They don't have money there."

Shea frowns. "What if he's not who you think he is?" she asks. "What if he's just an old bum?"

Before I can stop myself, my fist flies out and I punch her arm. She pulls back, surprised. "Never say that again," I hiss at her. "Never!"

"You hit me! Nobody hits me!" Shea jumps up, her face red.

I get up too, but she's already running into the woods, her back dappled with splashes of sunlight. "Come back," I call after her. "I'm sorry. I didn't hit you hard, it couldn't have hurt."

But she's already gone. I hear the faint sound of bushes rustling as she crashes through them and then nothing. I glance at the Green Man. He has one eye open, watching me.

"What happened, Brendan? Where did Shea go?"

I'm so ashamed that I turn away, unable to look at him while I tell him. "I hit her — I didn't mean to, and it wasn't a hard hit, just a sort of punch. But she ran off."

The Green Man sits up. A leaf falls out of his hair. "Why on earth did you hit her?"

"She said something that made me mad. Now she hates me."

"No, no, no." The Green Man pats my shoulder. "She'll get over it. She's not the sort to hate anyone. Nor is she the sort to stay mad long. Wait and see. She'll be fine tomorrow."

"Tomorrow's Saturday," I say. "She'll be gone all weekend with her family."

"Where's she going this time?"

"To Deep Creek Lake. Her father bought a kayak. She showed me a picture in the L.L. Bean catalog. It's red. She's going to learn how to paddle it."

The Green Man strokes his beard. "Lucky Shea."

"Yes," I say.

"Have you ever met Shea's family?" the Green Man asks.

"I've never even been to her house," I admit.

"Why not?"

I shrug and swat a mosquito making a meal of my blood. "She's never invited me."

"But she's your best friend."

"Well, she's never been to my house either."

"And why ever not?"

"Because Mrs. Clancy doesn't allow me to bring kids over when she's not there, and she's not home very much because she works at the card shop at the mall. Besides, she's grumpy. She probably wouldn't like Shea."

I hesitate. "Plus I told Shea I live with my mother just like an ordinary kid."

The Green Man scratches his belly and gazes into the woods, his face sad. "Why did you lie?" he asks slowly, as if he isn't sure he should pry into my life.

"Everybody thinks there's something wrong with foster kids. They have bad blood or something. I heard one of Mrs. Clancy's friends say that."

He shakes his head and puts an arm around my shoulder. "The world is full of small-minded people," he says. "There's nothing wrong with you, Brendan. You're fine."

I lean against him. He's big and solid and I feel safe with him. "You and Shea are the only friends I have," I say. "And now maybe I'm down to just you."

"It's late," he says after a while. "When does Mrs. Clancy come home?"

"Around seven," I tell him.

"Must be almost that now."

The Green Man and I walk together through the woods. I feel the animals gathering near us, deer and rabbits, foxes and squirrels, raccoons. I can't see them or hear them, but they hide in the underbrush and watch me walk by with the Green Man, the king of the forest. He's protecting me the way he protects them.

A train is coming, so we stop beside the tracks and watch it thunder past, shaking the rails with its weight, boxcars bouncing and swaying. When it's gone, the Green Man says goodbye and walks back into the woods.

In a second, he's gone. No twig snaps. No leaf rustles.

I think of what Shea said, and I know she's wrong. Only a true Green Man could vanish into the woods without a sound. He's magic. He is.

He must be.

ELEVEN

IT'S NOT MRS CLANCY'S SATURDAY to work, so I don't have to waste the day at the mall. I eat breakfast at six a.m., long before she gets up. Before I fell asleep last night, I made a plan. Once, I heard Shea tell Mr. Hailey she lived on Summer Hill Road. I don't know the house number, but I know where the street is. I figure I'll walk up and down the street, and if I'm lucky I'll see her before she leaves for Deep Creek Lake. I'll apologize for hitting her and forgive her for what she said about the Green Man.

I know where Summer Hill Road is because there's a Dairy Queen on the corner. Once in a while, if she's in a good mood, Mrs. Clancy stops there on the way home from the mall and buys us each a double swirl cone. Chocolate for her and vanilla for me. We sit on a picnic bench and watch people come and go. Mrs. Clancy doesn't want to get in the car until we're finished so I don't get ice cream on the upholstery.

It's a long walk, uphill, downhill all the way across town, along Route 22, a treeless road jammed with cars and trucks and buses belching fumes like dragons. I've never been so hot in my life. There's no escape from the sun or the smell of fast food frying in old grease, but I keep my feet moving by picturing the red kayak and the river. And Shea — seeing her, making up with her, being friends again.

The Dairy Queen is at the top of a hill, and by the time I get there my hair is a wet mop on the back of my neck, my T-shirt sticks to my skin, and I wish I had enough money to buy a soda. I think about going in and asking for some water, but I remember they charge you ten cents for the cup and I don't even have that.

Even if I had a dime, it wouldn't make any difference. The place isn't open yet.

I head down Summer Hill Road. The houses are little wood bungalows, exactly alike except for stuff people have done to them since they were built. Additions, different paint colors, screened-in porches, gardens, trellises. Some houses look really nice, others are in bad shape. Dirt or weeds instead of grass. Peeling paint. Overgrown bushes.

I keep expecting the neighborhood to change. Where are the big houses? Surely rich people don't live in places like this.

I come to another hill. I tell myself the houses on the other side will be fancy and I'll see Shea. But at the top of the hill, I stare down at a cluster of brick apartment buildings and rows of duplex houses. It's a dead end at the railroad tracks.

I can't think of any other Summer Hill but this one. I must have misunderstood the name of her street.

So I keep walking. What else is there to do? At the end of the street, I can follow the railroad tracks to the woods.

I pass the Summer Hill Gardens apartment complex but I don't see any gardens, just brown grass and a few lopsided bushes half dead from the heat. On the other side of the street are the duplex houses. One has a foreclosure sign in front. The weeds are so tall, I can't see the sidewalk. The windows have sheets of plywood nailed over them, spray-painted with gang tags. I can tell no one lives there anymore.

I see junked cars in yards, a refrigerator without a

door on someone's porch, rusty bikes and broken toys. Dogs bark and growl and lunge at the chainlink fences. One house has three signs on the gate: BEWARE OF DOG, GUARD DOG ON PREMISES, PRIVATE PROPERTY KEEP OUT. I wonder what they can possibly have in that house.

Then I see Shea. I stop and hide behind a telephone pole. She's standing on the porch of a rundown duplex, yelling at someone inside. "I'm not changing his diapers. He stinks. You're his mother — you do it!"

The screen door opens. A hand grabs Shea and yanks her inside. The door slams with a bang that echoes off the apartments across the street. Three or four dogs in the yard next door start barking.

A woman shouts at Shea. Shea shouts back. I can't understand what they're saying, but they're mad. A baby cries. A man opens the door and lets it slam behind him. *Bang.* It's like a gunshot. The dogs bark frantically. They race up and down the fence, snarling.

Someone inside the house yells, "Where are you going?"

"Out," the man hollers. He's red-faced from the heat. His T-shirt is dark with sweat under his arms. His jeans dip below his belly. Ignoring the shouts and wails behind him, he runs down the steps and jumps into an old truck.

Revving the engine, he backs down the driveway, turns toward Route 22, and passes me. I glimpse his face, tight with anger, and then he's gone.

I don't know what to do. I don't understand what I'm seeing. Nothing matches Shea's description of her house and family.

I stand behind the telephone pole and wait for something else to happen. The yelling in the house slowly subsides. The baby stops crying. The dogs next door curl up in the shade under the front porch. Heat prickles my skin. Sweat runs down my back. I think about cutting my hair. Maybe even shaving my head.

Finally the door opens. Shea comes out carrying a baby. A little girl follows her. Then a boy who's about seven. Shea dumps the baby in a stroller in the front yard and opens the gate. She walks toward me but she doesn't see me because she's talking to the little girl.

"Don't suck your thumb, Tessa. It makes you look stupid."

Tessa looks at Shea, but she keeps her thumb in her mouth.

Shea frowns. "Do you want to look stupid?"

Tessa stares at her feet. She's wearing frayed flip-flops and her T-shirt is stained with chocolate. "I hate you," she mutters.

I shift around the pole, trying to hide. I shouldn't have come here. Shea will be mad if she sees me.

The little boy stops and stares at me. "Who's that girl?" he asks Shea.

She stops dead. Her face turns red. "Brendan, what are you doing here?"

She looks at me as if I've committed a crime. Maybe I have. My guts are tied into big thick knots. She really hates me now. The dogs come out from under the porch and start barking again.

I back away, shaking my head, flapping my hands. I don't know what to say or what to do. "I . . ." I start. "I —"

Shea's grip on the stroller's handle tightens. Tessa sucks harder on her thumb. The boy glares at me. I wish a sinkhole would open in the sidewalk and I'd fall in, disappear, never see Shea again. I don't know which is worse — her finding me in front of her house or me discovering she's been lying all summer long.

The baby rocks back and forth in the stroller. He starts to cry. Tessa scowls at him. "Blubber blubber blubber," she says.

The dogs run up and down. One puts his front paws on top of the fence and growls at me.

"Shut up, Wolfie," Shea tells the dog. "Shut up, all of you!"

They keep on barking and running and leaping at the fence, and the boy tugs at Shea's hand, trying to loosen it from the stroller. "Come on, you said you were taking us to the park. Let's go!"

Without even looking at me, Shea pushes the stroller past. I don't know what else to do, so I follow her. She keeps her head high and her dark curls bounce. The boy says, "That girl's following us."

"He's not a girl. He just has long hair." Shea doesn't look back. She's pushing the stroller as fast as she can.

"He *looks* like a girl," the boy insists. This time Shea ignores him.

My face burns. Do I really look like a girl?

The park is at the end of the road. The train tracks run along one side of it. A few kids are playing baseball in the hot sun. I hear the bat hit the ball. Someone yells, "Easy catch!"

Shea heads for the slides and swings in the shade. From a distance, I watch her lift the baby out of the stroller. She fastens him into a plastic swing made for little kids and pushes him.

"'Wing," he shouts. "'Wing!"

"Push me," Tessa yells, and climbs into a swing next to the baby. Shea pushes them both. The boy swings himself, his skinny legs pumping him higher and higher.

I sit down on the bottom of the sliding board and wait to see what will happen next.

After a while, Shea takes the baby out of the swing, puts him back in the stroller, and sticks a bottle in his mouth. Tessa and the boy squat in the sandbox and dig holes with spoons Shea gives them. She looks at me. I look at her.

"What do you want?" she asks.

"I came to say I was sorry for hitting you yesterday."

"It didn't hurt," she says.

"That's good."

Shea doesn't answer. She sits on a bench and rocks the stroller with her foot, pushing it back and forth, back and forth. One wheel squeaks, but the baby falls asleep anyway. Shea stares into the spindly woods. We both know there's no magic in them. Or in this hot playground.

"I babysit Tessa and Cody and Shane every weekend," Shea says in a low voice, still avoiding my eyes. "They're my mother's kids with her second husband. My real dad died in Afghanistan."

"He got shot," the boy says. He leans against the picnic table and runs his finger around the initials carved there.

"Cody," Tessa yells, "come see what I'm making!"

Cody glances at me. "A stupid house for fairies probably. Girls are so dumb."

"Go on, Cody." Shea pokes him with the foot that's not pushing the stroller. "You'll wake up Shane."

I watch him walk over to a chinning bar and struggle to lift his skinny body high enough.

"So now you know," Shea says.

"Yes."

"There's no kayak, no weekend trips."

"No."

"I live in a crummy house. I hate my stepdad. I fight with my mother. I have three bratty half-sibs." She looks at Shane and sighs. "Before my daddy died, we really did live in Guam, but my stepdad's not in the army. We move a lot because he gets fired or quits or the company goes out of business or cuts the staff or something. It's never his fault."

Shea scoops her hair off the back of her neck and holds it on top of her head. "So," she says without looking at me. "Do you hate me now?"

"Why would I hate you?"

"Because I'm a liar."

I shrug. Now's the time. I have to tell her about me and my life. "I told you a bunch of lies too. I don't have any parents. Not a mother, not a father. My mother left me in the hospital after I was born and nobody knows her name. She just walked away. Nobody knows who my father is either. So I'm in foster care."

The words tumble out, falling over each other as I say them, but at least I've let them out of my head. I look up and meet Shea's eyes.

"What if your mother is looking for you? What if she's sorry she left you in the hospital?" She's very serious, I can tell. She wants to believe my mother will find me someday.

"I used to think the same thing," I tell her. "I imagined her going somewhere and looking up my birth certificate. If you know the place a person was born and the date, you can do that — even if you don't know the person's name. So she could find me if she wanted to." I pick up a stick and start breaking it into little pieces. *Snap snap snap.*

I look at Shea. "She doesn't want to find me. I was a mistake. Maybe I ruined her life. Maybe she met some guy and got married and she has a family now. Other kids. Maybe she doesn't even think of me."

"Maybe she has amnesia," Shea says. "Maybe she's dead and she died thinking of you and wishing she hadn't left you in the hospital."

Before I can tell Shea she watches too many movies,

she says, "Or maybe she's scared you hate her and that's why she doesn't come."

Of all the things Shea's said or I've thought, this makes the most sense. My mother's scared to see me, she thinks I hate her. Which I don't. I just want her to knock on Mrs. Clancy's door and tell me she's my mother and she's so, so sorry about abandoning me and we'll go away together and live in our own house in East Bedford so I can still be friends with Shea. I really thought I'd stopped hoping this would happen but here I am, just like the little kid I used to be, daydreaming about my mother.

"When you get older," Shea says, "you can get all the information from Social Services and go find your mother yourself. Somebody must know her name."

Shea goes on talking about how to find my mother, but my thoughts have drifted. What will I be like when I'm eighteen or twenty-one? I can't imagine myself that far in the future, but I'll probably be just like I am now, only even weirder. Or maybe not. Maybe I'll be an ordinary boring person living in the real world, dealing with Life. Will I have a job? Will I still love to draw or will I grow out of stuff like that? I don't like thinking about being eighteen or twenty-one. It scares me. I'd rather stay twelve forever like Peter Pan.

Shea punches my arm lightly. "You aren't listening to a word I'm saying, are you?"

I slide closer to her, close enough to smell her hair, sort of doggy in the heat. "You know what?" I say. "I'm glad we both lied. It makes us equal."

I smile at her and she smiles back. Propping my elbows on the picnic table, I stare across the field at the kids playing baseball. Now that I've told Shea everything, my chest feels looser. It's like I've been holding my breath ever since I met her, sure she'd stop being my friend if she knew about Mrs. Clancy. But it's okay. She's sitting here beside me just like always.

She scoops up her hair again and holds it on top of her head. "Why is it so hot?" she says.

"Maybe because it's summer?"

She laughs and I see the little gap between her front teeth. The scar on her cheek. Her funny cats' eyes.

Over in the sandbox, Cody and Tessa are quarreling.

"There are so fairies!" Tessa shouts.

"Have you ever seen one?" Cody's voice is scornful. If he's not careful, he'll grow up to be a real-lifer.

"Course I have."

"Liar."

Tessa's voice rises. "They live in the lilac bush in the backyard."

"Oh, sure." Cody gets up and walks back to the chinning bar.

"Stupid dummy! I seen them! I seen them with my own eyes," Tessa yells.

She wakes up Shane, who starts to cry until Shea plugs his mouth with a pacifier.

Shane spits it out and keeps crying. Shea picks it up, wipes the dirt off on her shirt, and sticks it back in his mouth. He spits it out again.

Tessa comes over and leans against Shea. "I'm hungry," she says.

Shea looks at the big watch she wears. "It's almost noon. I better take them home."

We walk back to her house. Cody asks me why my hair is so long. I say I like it that way. "My dad says only potheads wear their hair long. Do you smoke pot?"

"Of course he doesn't," Shea answers for me. "You are so rude, Cody."

"I just want to know stuff," Cody says. "Hey," he yells at a boy on a bike. "Give me a ride, Danny!"

The boy stops, and Cody hops on the handlebars. They zoom away downhill.

"He's going to get himself killed someday," Shea says.

When we pass the house with the dogs, they run

out from under the porch and start barking and leaping again.

"Do they do that every time you pass their fence?" I ask.

Shea nods. "They're bored. No one takes them for walks or pays any attention to them. They spend every day in that yard with nothing to do but bark. Some life, huh?"

Shea's mother is sitting on the front porch reading a magazine. Her hair's long and dark like Shea's and she's wearing shorts and a red T-shirt. She's really pretty, more like a teenager than the mother of four kids.

"Back already?" she asks.

Tessa opens the gate and runs to her mother. "I'm hungry. I want a peanut butter sandwich with strawberry jam. Can I? Please please please?"

"Ask Shea. She'll fix it for you."

"I want you to fix it!"

At that moment, the pickup truck pulls into the driveway. The stepdad doesn't look any happier than he did when he left the house. This time he notices me.

"Looks like you picked up another stray," he says to Shea. "Better take her back where you found her. We have enough mouths to feed already." He laughs like he's kidding, but I decide it's time to leave.

"He's not a girl," Cody tells his father. "He's a boy with long hair. But not a pothead."

But the man has already lost interest in me. The screen door bangs shut behind him. The baby starts to cry and the dogs start to bark.

"Can you get away Sunday?" I whisper to Shea.

She shakes her head. "See you Monday," she says. "Don't forget your math homework."

I wave goodbye and head down the street toward the train tracks. It's so hot, the tracks waver in the distance. I smell creosote oozing out of the railroad ties. I inhale it, filling my nose with its pungent odor. It's a summer smell and I love it.

TWELVE

WHILE I WALK, I think about Shea's life and how different it is from what I imagined. Sad, it's sad — her life, my life too. How come some kids are lucky and others aren't?

There's this kid in my school. He was born with something wrong with his spine, and he'll never be able to walk. And he's not the only one. Our school has a wing set aside for kids like him. At least he's smart and funny and he loves to read. Others are less lucky. They can't talk, they can't even sit up. It's not fair, is it? There's something wrong with this so-called real world.

I want to talk to the Green Man about it. He's been around for so many years. Maybe he can explain it.

But when I finally reach my tree, I don't see him. I

wait awhile just in case he appears, but I'm tired and I'm thirsty and I'm hungry and I'm hot. So I go home.

Mrs. Clancy is watching a game show on TV. "Where have you been all day?" she asks.

"Just out," I say, and head for the kitchen.

"If you'd been home at noon, I'd have fixed your lunch," she calls over the din of a commercial, "but it's after two."

I open the refrigerator and get out bread and cheese and mustard. "Don't make a mess out there," she calls.

"I won't." I fix my sandwich, grab a bottle of water, and sit down to eat. Today's paper is lying on the table, so I scan the front page: THREE SOLDIERS KILLED BY SUI-CIDE BOMBER IN AFGHANISTAN. CAR CRASH LEAVES FIVE DEAD. ARSON SUSPECTED IN APARTMENT FIRE. LOCAL POLITICIAN ARRESTED FOR DUI.

The same stuff happens day after day, week after week, year after year after year. All that changes are the names and the dates. Depressed, I turn to the crossword puzzle, but Mrs. Clancy has already done most of it. I fill in the words she didn't know and make some correc-tions.

I think about going back to the woods, but I doubt the Green Man will be there. Besides, Mrs. Clancy has decided we need to go to Costco. She's got a long list of stuff to buy, including new underwear for me. Why can't I stay home and read, I ask, but she just clamps her lips together and ushers me to the car. *No telling what you'll do if I leave you home alone,* she's thinking.

Actually, it's good I go, because she's in a nice mood and buys me three T-shirts and a pair of jeans along with the boring underwear. She even treats me to a soda.

On Sunday morning, I wake up to the sound of thunder and hard wind-driven rain blowing in my open window. Half asleep, I slam the window shut and use an old T-shirt to mop up the water on the floor. Mrs. Clancy is always telling me not to leave the windows open at night, but I, of course, am a careless, irresponsible, thoughtless boy whose reason for existence is to make Mrs. Clancy miserable.

When the floor is dry, I wad up the T-shirt and shove it under my bed along with all the other junk I've kicked under there on room-cleaning days. Maybe she won't notice it's missing. After all, I have three new ones to wear now.

In the kitchen, Mrs. Clancy is sitting at the table reading the newspaper and sipping coffee. "It's about time you honored me with your presence," she says — her way of greeting me. Yesterday's good mood is gone.

I grab a bowl and dump cereal into it.

"Are you going to eat all that?" she asks. "You know how I hate it when you waste food."

She's in rare form today. Instead of answering, I pour on milk and fill a glass with orange juice. "How was the bingo game last night?"

"Can't you see I'm reading the paper?"

Badly, I think. It went badly. "Can I have the comics?"

She slides them across the table. "I wouldn't waste my time reading comics. You'll rot your brain."

Silently I read my favorites, finish my cereal, and wish I had something to do besides spend the day in the house with my loving foster mother. "Can I borrow an umbrella?" I ask.

"*May* I borrow an umbrella," she corrects me.

"May I borrow an umbrella, please?" I tack on *please* because she'll say something about the magic word if I don't.

"What do you want it for?"

To hold over my head while I take a shower, I think, *to keep from getting a sunburn,* but out loud I say, "I need to go to the library. My history report's due tomorrow."

Without remembering that the library's closed on

Sundays, she says, "Take the one hanging on the hook by the back door. And don't lose it. It's my best one."

Outside I take a deep breath of pure joy and head for the convenience store at the Sunoco station. Rain drums on the umbrella and splashes in puddles on the sidewalk. I have enough money to buy a soda and a twelve-inch Italian sub to eat for lunch. If the Green Man shows up, I can split the sub with him.

While I'm waiting to pay, Sean and his thugs come into the store. They have their sweatshirt hoods over their heads to keep the rain off. They look as big and scary and mean as ever, and they're laughing in a nasty way about something that probably isn't even funny.

Hoping they won't notice me, I turn my back and hand the cashier my money. I notice she's keeping an eye on them. She probably knows who they are.

I grab my change. I want to get out of there before they see me. Or rob the store and maybe shoot the poor girl at the cash register.

Half running, half walking, I head down the train tracks toward the woods. The rain has stopped but it's still cloudy, like it might start again any second.

In a few minutes, I hear voices behind me. It's them. I walk faster.

"The stupid girl never saw a thing," one says.

"She sure was looking, though." They laugh.

"Gimme some of the potato chips."

It sounds like they're catching up with me. Just as I'm thinking I should disappear into the woods, Sean says, "Hey, isn't that the long-haired freaky kid?"

Gene laughs and says, "I thought it was a girl."

"He's the one who told the cops about us," T.J. says. "I ran right past the little punk."

I start scrambling up the embankment toward the woods, but the cinders are wet and slippery from the rain and I fall. Before I can get up, I'm surrounded. Sean yanks me to my feet. He and T.J. drag me into the woods. Gene grabs the bag from the convenience store and Mrs. Clancy's umbrella.

"Look at this," he says, "the freak brought us lunch. Isn't that nice of him? Or her?"

"And an umbrella in case it starts raining again." T.J. opens the umbrella and dances around, spinning it madly.

By the time he's finished, Mrs. Clancy's umbrella is inside out, the struts are broken, the fabric is torn. "Man," he says, "they just don't make umbrellas like they used to." With that, he hurls it up in the air several times until he succeeds in tangling it in a tree's branches.

The boys keep me surrounded while they eat my sandwich and drink my soda. The woods are very still. Water drips from the trees, and the air is heavy with humidity. A crow caws from a branch over my head and flies like a black arrow into the dense foliage. He's gone to fetch the Green Man. He'll rescue me from this band of varlets, these intruders.

The boys throw their trash on the ground. Gene pulls out a bottle of whiskey and they pass it around. They talk in low voices and laugh. A dragon tattoo on Sean's neck moves every time Sean turns his head. T.J. goes off into the woods and comes back zipping his fly. They light cigarettes and mutter to each other.

Just when I think they've forgotten about me, T.J. looks my way. "What should we do with him?" he asks Sean.

All three of them stare at me through the smoke. The bottle is almost empty, and I don't like the look in their eyes. I back away but it's too late. Sean grabs me. "Let's do him a favor and give him a haircut."

They put their cigarettes out. Gene swallows the last of the whiskey. T.J. yanks me to my feet and pins my arms behind my back. Sean pulls a knife out of his motorcycle boot. It has a long, wicked blade.

I try to get away, but Sean hacks off a long clump of

my hair. If I fight, I might get my scalp sliced or my ears cut off, so, with my head down, I stand still and let him chop off all my hair, right down to the scalp. My head stings from the nicks he makes in my skin, and my hair litters the ground at my feet. *C* is for *curl*, *C* is for *cut*, *C* is for *cruel*.

"There." Sean steps back and studies his work "Isn't that better?"

"Now he looks like a bald girl," Gene says. "Even uglier than before."

"A punk skinhead," T.J. says. "Maybe I should give him a few tattoos. An iron cross, maybe." He sticks his arm in my face. The iron cross is crude, he probably did it himself. There's a skull and crossbones on his upper arm. That's even worse.

I flinch, terrified they might cover me with neo-Nazi tattoos.

Sean shakes his head. "We got stuff to do, T.J. We don't have time to give the punk a tattoo." He shoves his face close to mine and brandishes the knife under my nose. "You told the cops about us, didn't you?"

"No, no, I didn't." My voice shakes. I sound like a girl, a child, a baby. "I never said anything. They talked to lots of people. I saw the cops writing stuff down."

"You freak. You gave them our names." Sean yanks

out a hunk of hair he'd missed. The pain sears my scalp.

T.J. crowds in, closer even than Sean. "I ran past you and you looked right at me. You knew who I was. And you told the cops."

"No," I whisper. "No."

"They don't have anything on us yet, but they're sniffing around," Sean tells me. "Somebody told."

"It was you, you freaky long-haired moron." Gene shoves me so hard I fall down.

T.J. drags me to my feet. "Even if you haven't told nobody yet, you might tell now."

"Let's teach the lying punk a lesson."

They jump me, all three of them. They hit me, pound me with their fists. My nose spouts blood. They knock me down and kick me. Three against one.

There's nothing I can do. I lie on the wet ground, curled into a ball, my hands over my head, and hope they won't kill me.

While they pound me into the ground, I cry out silently for the Green Man. *Where are you? Why haven't you come? These are your woods, your kingdom, you're supposed to protect me, to keep me safe from my enemies.*

The woods are silent. He doesn't come. He doesn't care what happens to me.

At last the beating stops.

"Keep your ugly lying mouth shut," Sean says. He's still holding the knife. The point touches my throat. I feel its sharpness. "It'll be worse next time."

I shake my head. *No, I won't tell, I won't*. I get to my feet slowly and back away. I trip over a log and fall flat on my back in the wet leaves. "Don't let me see you again," Sean says.

I hear them walk away, laughing. They're done with me for now. I don't get up. I lie where I've fallen and stare up into the trees.

"Where are you?" I call to the Green Man. There's no answer. Just the sound of my own voice echoing back from the trees.

I don't know how long I lie there in the wet leaves waiting for him to come, making up excuses for him, certain he will come, he must come. But he doesn't come.

As the day turns to evening, I try to get up. It hurts to move. Maybe I'll just lie here, die here. Maybe someone will find my bones someday. Mrs. Clancy will be sorry then, she'll wish she'd treated me better. *That boy,* she'll say, *he wasn't so bad after all. If only I'd been nicer to him.*

And the Green Man. He'll blame himself for ignoring my pleas. *Ah, the poor lad,* he'll think, *gone from this world before his time, and it's all my fault. Why didn't I go to him? Why didn't I protect him?*

And Sean and T.J. and Gene — they will go to prison for the rest of their lives.

The ground under me grows colder and damper. Maybe I don't want to die here after all. I struggle to stand and stumble away through the woods. I fall and trip and stagger. I've never been so weak. I've never hurt so bad.

By the time I get to my tree, I've given up hope of seeing the Green Man. I fall to the ground, exhausted. I ache all over. My ribs, my belly, my scalp. My heart, my soul. The Green Man has abandoned me. I'm all alone. Like always. Why did I think the Green Man would be different?

I don't have the strength to climb up to my platform, so I curl up on the damp ground and shut my eyes. I try to sleep, but Sean's face keeps flashing on and off like a strobe light. He hits me again and again, he kicks me, I feel the pain of my hair being hacked off. I hear Sean and his friends cursing me, jeering. It's like it's happening over and over and over.

I must fall asleep, because the next thing I know it's almost dark. I get to my feet like an old man, stiff and aching with pain. The Green Man hasn't come. I'm still alone.

I look at the blood on my shirt. I feel the itchy stubble on my head. How am I going to explain this to Mrs. Clancy? I've lost her best umbrella. My shirt is ruined. She'll be furious. *You stupid boy, I told you not to lose that umbrella. Look at your shirt, what happened to your hair? You look like a freak, you are a freak. I can't keep you here any longer, I'm calling Social Services first thing in the morning.*

With Mrs. Clancy's voice ringing in my head, I climb slowly and painfully up the tree. I won't go to her house. I'll stay here in the woods, where I belong.

I drink from a bottle of water stashed in a milk crate and find a box of stale crackers. I eat them all, but they don't fill my belly.

The moon sails in and out of clouds. The wind blows and rocks my platform like a cradle and I hope the bough doesn't break. The rain begins again. Cold and miserable, I crawl under the tarp, cover myself with my smelly old blanket, and lie down to sleep. The boards under me are uneven. They press against the sore parts of me. My belly rumbles, my cuts and bruises throb, my head feels too small for my body. I'm the Ancient Mariner, cursed and alone.

Deep in the woods, an owl screeches, not a gentle

too-whit-too-woo but a scream, a shriek, loud and harsh and scary, like someone being murdered. I pull the blanket over my head, but the owl keeps screaming. A coyote yips and howls in the distance, and a dog barks back. Branches crack and limbs creak. Wind rustles the leaves. Rain drips through the tarp.

I wake up every hour or so, hungry and sore. I drink more water. I pee off the edge of the platform. The rain stops and the sky slowly lightens. Birds sing. A fresh breeze blows through the treetops. The woods are a familiar place again.

But something's missing. The woods are just woods after all. There's nothing special or magical about them. Trees, just trees, that's all I see now. Ordinary, real-life trees.

In the gray morning light, I look at all the dumb things I've made. One by one, I tear up my drawings and scatter them like flakes of snow. I keep my swords and shields and lances in case I need to defend myself, but I hurl my carvings of the Green Man as far away as I can. I never want to see them or him again. I was foolish to believe in myths and legends, to think he was anything but an old man pretending to be what I wanted him to be. I should have listened to Shea instead of getting angry.

I sit on the edge of the platform and peer down.

Torn drawings are scattered on the ground or caught in branches. A bit of the Green Man here, a piece of Lady Shea there, shreds of knights and dragons, elves and fairies, castles and ogres—nothing now but scraps of paper.

My heart's a heavy lump in my chest. My arms and legs hurt, my head aches, even my belly is sore from the beating.

I search my tree house for food. While I'm rummaging in my art box, thinking I might find a stale Twinkie hidden there, I come across a jar of green tempera paint. Suddenly I know what to do. I dump the paint in a bucket and add water until it's about the consistency of cream. I yank off my clothes and throw them away. Like my drawings, they flutter down into the trees. Only my shoes make it all the way to the ground. Taking a deep breath, I smear the watery paint all over myself. Even though it stings, I rub it into my bald head with particular care.

When the paint's gone, I'm green all over, or at least as much of me as I can reach. I wrap a rag around myself like a loincloth. I make a crown of leaves. Since I have no hair, my ears hold it up. With the aid of Shea's mirror, I paint designs on my face. I don't recognize the warrior I see in the mirror. I'm a savage now, a wild boy, strong and brave and fearless.

"The Green Man is dead!" I shout. "Long live the Green Man!"

My voice echoes back from trees and rocks. I, Brendan Doyle, have proclaimed myself the Spirit of the Forest, the true Green Man. I shall dwell here the rest of my life. I shall protect the birds and the beasts and the fish that swim in the streams. I shall protect the trees.

I'll live on berries and roots. My hair will grow back, long and matted. I'll wear rags and tatters of clothing. I'll roam through the forest all the way down to Georgia, protecting birds and beasts. I'll become a legend. There will be sightings. People will search the forest, hoping to get a photograph of me.

But nobody will find me. I'll be safe.

Down below, I hear the bushes rustle softly. Someone is coming. I drop flat on my belly. If it's the Green Man, I won't answer when he calls. If it's Shea, she'll climb up here whether I answer or not.

THIRTEEN

B EFORE HE SPEAKS, his cough gives him away. "Brendan, my lad, are you up there?"

I lie still. Silent. Motionless. Invisible to anyone below.

He calls again. Then again. At last he says to himself, "Ah, he's in summer school, that's right. Bless me, I forgot."

From the noises I hear, I know he's settling down to stay awhile. Soon he's snoring.

I lean over the edge of my platform and look down. I see an old man in dirty clothes lying on his back in the weeds. His hair is tangled and long and uncombed, his beard shaggy and stained. The soles of his shoes are worn through in places.

With new eyes, I recognize him for what he is. A bum. And, even worse, a liar for letting me believe he was the Green Man.

Hours pass. No matter how I lie, on my right side or my left side, on my back or my belly, I hurt. The sun shines down through the leaves, stabbing my eyes with shifting brightness. Mosquitoes buzz around my itchy head. Gnats go after my ears and eyes.

At last I hear Shea trying to sneak through the bushes and not succeeding. She's as clumsy as an elephant's child.

"Well, little lady," the Green Man says. "What are you doing without your partner in crime?"

"He wasn't in school this morning." I imagine Shea biting her thumbnail the way she does when she's puzzled or worried. "We were supposed to hand in our history reports today. He was doing his on the Battle of Gettysburg. Mine was on Antietam." I hear Shea sit down. "Where do you think he is?"

"Maybe he was sick today."

"He never gets sick."

"Everybody gets sick." As if to prove it, he coughs a horrible loose cough.

"I guess."

Very cautiously, I peer over the edge of my platform.

Shea's sitting in the grass, her dark hair pulled back in a curly ponytail. Just as I thought, she's chewing her thumbnail and frowning.

The Green Man sits beside her. "Did you happen to bring any refreshments?" he asks Shea.

She opens her backpack and pulls out half a sandwich and an apple. "I brought extra for Brendan. He's always hungry."

"You're a good friend."

Shea picks up a stone and throws it at a tree. *Thunk.* It hits the target. "I told him a pack of lies about my family and the great stuff we do on weekends," she says in a low voice. "Saturday, he came to my house and found out the truth about me and my family and the dumpy house we live in. He said it was okay, he lied to me too, but maybe he's mad now. Maybe he hates me."

Shea sounds so sad that I'm tempted to call down and tell her I'm not mad at her, but I just lie there and say nothing. I don't want to have anything to do with the Green Man. Not now, not ever. He's a liar and a fake and a dirty old bum.

"Sometimes a lie starts by accident," the Green Man says, "and before long it's too late to admit it's not true."

"You know all about lying, don't you?" Shea asks.

"You aren't the Green Man. I saw you once in the park with those homeless men. You were drinking whiskey out of a paper bag."

I draw in my breath so hard, I almost choke. So it's true, I'm right. He's a liar and a bum.

The Green Man coughs, but he doesn't deny what Shea has said.

"At first I thought you just looked like the man in the park," Shea goes on. "When you stole that bottle of beer, I knew you weren't the Green Man. But Brendan believed it with his whole heart and soul. Why did you let him?"

He shakes his head. "I believed it was a game and my part was to be the Green Man. I didn't think Brendan really and truly believed I was a supernatural hero of some sort."

"Well, he did," Shea says. There's an angry edge in her voice. "And so did I — for a while."

The Green Man lowers his head. "It was a lovely game," he says sadly. "I don't know what Brendan will think of me if he finds out I'm just an ordinary old man."

I jump to my feet, a wooden sword in my hand. "I already know the truth!" I shout at him. "Go away from here. I never want to see you again!"

They both look up at me, startled, then shocked.

"Where are your clothes?" Shea stares up at me. "What happened to your hair? And your skin? You've turned green."

"You're hurt." The Green Man struggles to his feet. "Come down from that tree and let us help you. You look terrible."

"I don't need your help!" I shout. "*I'm* the Green Man now. The true Green Man!"

"Brendan, please come down," Shea begs. "He's right, you're hurt."

Is Shea on *his* side now? Is she a traitor too? My head hurts, my heart hurts, my whole body hurts. I'm so hungry that I'm dizzy. But I'm not climbing down there. They can't make me. Even if Shea climbs up here, she can't make me come down. Unless she pushes me off the edge, and I don't think she'd do that.

"Brendan," the Green Man calls. "I know you're angry with me, but I never meant to hurt you. I thought we were playing a game."

Pretend. That's all it was to him. A game little kids play in the woods. Maybe Shea never believed it either. I have no friends after all. Only enemies.

Shea looks at the drawings ripped to pieces and scattered everywhere. She picks up a crumpled sheet of paper and smoothes it. "Oh, Brendan, you tore up your pictures."

"So what if I did?" I wave my sword. "You aren't Princess Shea and he's not the Green Man. It's all kid stuff, not worth anything."

"But I'm still your friend," Shea says. "I'll always be your friend. Even if you hate me."

The Green Man runs his fingers through his beard, straightening it, getting rid of a few tangles. He doesn't look at me.

Shea approaches the tree. "I'm coming up there," she says.

"Don't you dare." I brandish my sword. "This is my tree now. I shouldn't have let you climb up here. You're a traitor just like him!"

"I'm not a traitor." Shea disappears into the hollow trunk, and I hear her scrabbling up. Soon she's on a branch, hitching herself higher hand over hand, feet walking up the tree trunk.

"You can't make me come down," I tell her. "You can't make me do anything."

She studies me. "Why did you cut off your hair and paint yourself green? Who gave you that black eye? And how did you get those cuts and scratches and bruises? Have you been in a fight?"

I scowl at her, trying hard to hate her, trying hard to stay angry. "It's none of your business."

"Where are your clothes?" Shea sounds embarrassed. "You can't go around half naked."

"I don't need them anymore. I don't need you, either. Or him."

Shea turns away from me and sits on the edge of the platform, swinging her legs. She doesn't say anything for a while. I can't tell if she's mad or worried or what. Maybe she's embarrassed because of my loincloth.

I retreat silently to the opposite side of the platform and sit with my back to her. I'm beginning to feel embarrassed myself.

Finally she says, "Did you sleep here last night?"

I pretend she's not here. I pretend *he's* not here. It's just me and the Green Wood. My kingdom now.

"I bet you're hungry," Shea says.

I don't answer.

"I'm sorry I gave my sandwich to the Green Man," she says softly. "If I'd known you were here—"

I can't ignore her any longer. "I wouldn't have eaten it anyway," I tell her. "I don't want anything from you."

I glance at her over my shoulder. She's still sitting on the edge of the platform, swinging her skinny legs. Sunlight splashes her shirt with shifting patterns. Without looking at me, she asks, "Does Mrs. Clancy know where you are?"

"I'm never going near her house again."

Shea looks at me then, a long, hard stare. "What do you plan to do? Live in the woods like some kind of crazy boy?"

"I'm not a crazy boy! I just want to live here all by myself." *Crazy*—why did she use that word? Does she think I'm crazy? Now I'm really angry.

"I just meant—" Shea begins, but I cut her off.

"I don't care what you meant! Leave me alone and don't tell anyone where I am."

"Brendan," the Green Man calls, "stop behaving like a jackass and come down here."

"Go away," I tell them. "Go away." I sit down and hide my head in my arms. I'm scared, I'm tired, I'm hungry, and I hurt all over.

Shea gets to her feet and comes over to kneel beside me. "Let's go to Mr. Hailey's house. He'll know what to do. His wife's a nurse."

I hesitate. "How do you know so much about Mr. Hailey and his wife? What makes you think they'd want me to show up at their door?"

"I was out with Tessa once," Shea says, "and we walked down his street, only I didn't know it was his street, and there he was, cutting the grass. It was hot, so he invited us in for a cold drink and I met his wife and she was wearing a nurse's uniform to go to work."

Shea takes my hand and tries to pull me to my feet. "Please, Brendan," she says. "You look like Tessa when she's coming down with something."

I resist, still not sure. Part of me longs to stay here in the woods, but another part longs to go with Shea. I'm tired and achy, and my brain feels muddled, as if my head is full of sand or something. I don't want to spend another night in the woods with no food. Like Shea says, I must be getting sick. That's what's wrong with me.

Finally I stop fighting and let her pull me to my feet. My legs have turned to spaghetti. I'm so dizzy I can't tell if it's the tree house or the woods that's spinning. I'm not sure I can climb down from the tree without falling.

With Shea ahead of me, I inch my way toward the ground, slowly, carefully.

The Green Man is waiting for me. He looks at my loincloth and says, "You can't go anywhere looking like that."

He retrieves my underwear and jeans, but he can find only one shoe. And no socks.

"Eeee-yu." Shea hands me my T-shirt. "It's got blood all over it and it stinks."

My underwear's not very fresh either. My jeans are so filthy, I hate to think what Mrs. Clancy will say when she sees them.

"You are a sad sight, Brendan." The Green Man comes closer and lays his big hand on my forehead. "You're burning up with fever, boy."

Without another word, he hoists me on his back and carries me piggyback.

I hold on tight and bury my face in the nape of his neck. I breathe in his familiar woodsy smell, I feel the texture of his curly hair against my cheek.

"Where were you? Why didn't you rescue me?" I whisper in his ear. "I called and I called but you didn't come. You didn't hear me and I was so scared. I thought they'd kill me and you wouldn't save me, you didn't care."

"Oh, Brendan, Brendan, I'm so sorry." The Green Man slows to a stop and stands still. His shoulders sag. "I'm a foolish old man. I never meant to trick you into thinking I was more than I am."

"I wanted you to be him so badly."

"I know that now." He sighs and his chest rattles. "I don't blame you for being angry, but I hope you'll forgive me."

I close my eyes and hug him. I'm too tired to talk anymore.

Shea turns and looks back. "Come on," she calls. "We have to get Brendan to Mr. Hailey's house."

The Green Man huffs and puffs behind her, but he won't let me walk. I'm too weak, he says, and I know he's right.

As we leave the grove, I look back at my tree. Will I ever see it again? The Green Man might be a phony, magic might be a fantasy, but I love my tree anyway.

I close my eyes, and the Green Man coughs and lurches through the woods with me on his back.

By the time we get to Mr. Hailey's, I'm in a sort of waking nap or dream. The supposed real world is soft and fuzzy and out of focus. Houses tilt this way and that. The sky seems very close. I actually reach out to touch a cloud, but as soon as I do, it moves out of reach. The birds are too big and their songs are so loud, they hurt my ears. I'm freezing cold and then I'm boiling hot.

Mr. Hailey opens the door, but he wavers as if he's made of smoke and then disappears, along with his house and yard. *Poof.* Everything disappears and I'm falling down down down into nowhere.

The next thing I know, I'm lying on a sofa in his house, and Mrs. Hailey is washing my face.

Shea is sitting near me, biting her thumbnail. Mr. Hailey is talking to the Green Man. Once in a while Shea says something, but all I hear are bits and pieces of conversation. I can't make much sense of anything they say. *Badly beaten . . . Night in the woods . . . Painted himself . . . Green Man . . . foster mother . . . hysterical . . . Missing child report . . . Police looking for him . . . Doesn't want to go home . . .*

"That's right," I say. "I'm going to live in the woods. All by myself." I try to sit up but fall back on my pillow. What's wrong with me? Why am I so weak? I must be really sick.

"Take it easy, Brendan," Mr. Hailey says. "We've called your foster mother, and she's on her way."

"No, no," I whisper. "She'll be mad. They broke her umbrella, my clothes are ruined, I lost one of my shoes. . . . She'll send me back to Social Services, maybe even the detention center."

But it's too late. A car pulls into the driveway, and a minute later Mrs. Clancy is standing over me. "Oh, my lord," she says, "I've been so worried. What happened to you? Where have you been? Just look at your poor head."

Without giving me a chance to answer, she pulls me up from the sofa. To my amazement, she hugs me. A quick, hard hug and then, "What were you thinking? Do you know how mortifying it is to tell the police your child is missing? How many questions they ask? I even got calls from Social Services."

She keeps on talking as she leads me outside. My head feels like it's going to float away, and I can barely stand up. Mr. Hailey helps get me into the car. He and Mrs. Hailey, Shea, and the Green Man stand in the driveway and wave until I can't see them anymore.

"Who was that scruffy girl?" Mrs. Clancy asks. "And that man—I've seen him in the park. He's a bum. A wino. What was he doing at Mr. Hailey's house?"

I slide down in the seat and rest my head against the window. The town glides by. Mrs. Clancy's voice is the soundtrack, and the streets and houses are a movie without a plot. A documentary, maybe. It should be in black-and-white.

"Don't you have anything to say?"

I shake my head and mumble something about not feeling good.

"I guess not," she says. "Have you had anything to eat?"

"Not hungry."

"Chicken soup with rice, that's what you need. Some applesauce, crackers, ginger ale. Hot tea with honey."

I don't say anything. She knows I don't eat meat. Why can't she remember? I'm too tired to explain. I just want to go to bed. And sleep for a week.

FOURTEEN

As soon as we get to her house, Mrs. Clancy fixes a hot bath for me and tells me to wash all the paint off before my cuts get infected.

"I'd do it myself," she says, "but you're too old for me to be bathing you."

After she shuts the door, I sink down into the tub. The water slowly turns muddy green. I wash languidly. Too weak to scrub. Too weak to drown myself.

"Your pajamas are on the chair in the hall," she shouts through the door. "Don't stay in there too long. You'll get a chill."

I get out of the tub and look at myself. I'm scratched and bruised all over. My head is covered with cuts and little tufts of hair that Sean missed. I look like what I am — an orphan no one loves or cares about. A lost boy from a Dickens novel. I wonder if my mother would have left me in the hospital if she'd known what my life would be like without her.

My mother. Why did I think of her? Has she ever thought of me? Probably she's forgotten me completely. *No, I never had a baby,* I can hear her say. Maybe to a doctor. Maybe to a friend. Maybe to her husband if she has one. Or to me, if I ever found her. *Don't you think I'd remember something like that?*

I shove my mother back into the box where I keep her, way down in a dark corner of my mind, and put on my pajamas.

Mrs. Clancy calls from the kitchen, "Your soup's ready," but I don't answer. I go into my room, shut the door, and crawl into bed. It's only five o'clock. The sun is shining. But all I want to do is sleep.

Mrs. Clancy has other ideas. Without even knocking, she barges into my room with a tray and sets it down on the bureau beside my bed. "Soup," she says. "Applesauce. Toast. Ginger ale."

I turn my head away and refuse to answer.

She sits down on the bed. The mattress sags under her weight. "Do I have to feed this to you?"

I don't say a word.

"Oh, Brendan," she sighs. "I'm too damned old for this nonsense. I don't have the energy to deal with you. I'm leaving the soup here. Eat it or not. It's vegetable noodle. No meat."

She stands up and walks away. She shuts the door behind her. Not with an angry bang but with a sort of sad thud.

Vegetable noodle . . . Did she remember after all? I sit up. My body aches with the effort. But I eat the soup and the toast and the applesauce. I drink the ginger ale. Then I lie down and listen to the birds singing in the maple tree. Sunlight stripes the wall. I hear the television. Mrs. Clancy is watching one of those women talk shows she loves. She told me once that her biggest disappointment in life was never seeing *The Oprah Winfrey Show* live. Especially the time she gave everybody cars. That's enough to make a person cry.

I pick up my battered copy of *The Return of the King*, but I'm too tired to read it. My eyes close and I sleep.

I dream I'm in a forest, not my forest but a truly ancient forest. The trees are so tall that I can't see their tops. Masses of leaves and branches hide the sky. In the dim light, I glimpse creatures moving through the forest, almost hidden by gigantic ferns. Trolls with misshapen bodies and huge heads, long arms dangling, some carrying cudgels, some carrying swords. They mustn't see me. I crouch down, hold my breath, but one stops and sniffs. The others pause. They sniff too. They talk in grumbles and growls, ugly sounds that mean nothing good. Then they begin crashing through the underbrush, trampling the ferns, huge, hairy-chested trolls heading straight for me.

I scramble to my feet, I try to run, I try to call for help, but my legs won't work and I can't speak. I stumble and thrash about, but I can't escape. They surround me. They have long, sharp yellow teeth. Their eyes are small and red. They jeer and laugh like dogs barking. They poke and prod, they push me around, they knock me down, they kick me. *Harf, harf,* they laugh. Louder and louder until the forest rings with the sound. *HARF! HARF!*

I try to call the Green Man but my voice is the cry of a mouse and it makes them laugh louder. *HARF! HARF!*

But then I hear someone running through the ferns, *swish swish*. Hands grasp my shoulders. It's him, I know it's him—he's come. This time he won't let me down. But the hands on my shoulders are small and weak. It's a dwarf, too old and feeble to help me. Or himself.

"Brendan, wake up!" I open my eyes and see Mrs. Clancy's face hanging over me. "You're having a bad dream!"

I'm in my room, in my bed, the sheets twisted around me, moonlight casting dark shadows on the wall. The forest is gone. The trolls are gone. The dwarf is gone. It's just Mrs. Clancy and me. The neighbor's dog is barking.

Still halfway between sleeping and waking, I stare around me, afraid I'll see the trolls huddled together in a dark corner, waiting for her to leave so they can drag me away. "The trolls," I mumble, "the trolls, they . . ."

"I thought someone was murdering you in your bed," she says. "Such screaming. A real fright you gave me."

Even in my sleep I can make her mad.

She lays her hand on my forehead. "You still feel feverish," she says. "I'll call the doctor tomorrow and have her look at you. I'm worried about those cuts getting infected. Why did you smear that green stuff all over you? Don't you ever think?"

I think all the time, *all* the time, every second, the thoughts in my head never leave me alone. But I don't tell her this. What's the point? She wouldn't understand.

"It's the middle of the night," she says. "We'll talk about this tomorrow. Go back to sleep."

She leaves the room without shutting the door. Before long, I hear her snoring. I wonder if she knows she does it. If I tell her, she'll probably deny it and get mad.

I turn on my light and read until I fall asleep.

The next day, Mrs. Clancy takes me to see Dr. Phillips. She's a pediatrician, and she's been my doctor ever since I came to East Bedford. I'm naturally very healthy, so I see her once a year for my school checkup, which never takes too long. Sometimes she asks me questions, but I never tell her much. I like to keep our discussions to my weight and height, stuff of an impersonal nature.

First she takes my temperature — 102. After that, she cleans my cuts carefully and rubs an antiseptic salve into them. She stitches up a couple of the worst ones. Next she gives me a shot of penicillin and a tetanus booster. I hate shots, but I try not to wince when she jabs a needle into my right arm and then into my left arm.

Last of all, she sits me down at her desk and asks me who beat me up and why I rubbed paint all over myself.

I look down at my hands. Just as I feared, we're not sticking to my height and weight.

"Brendan." She leans across her desk to get my attention. "This is serious. You've been badly beaten. Whoever hurt you should be arrested and charged."

I shake my head. "I don't know their names."

"Why did they attack you?"

"I have no idea. They just did, that's all. Maybe they didn't like my hair."

She knows I know more than I'm saying. But she can't make me tell.

"Did they threaten to hurt you if you told?"

I stare at her medical certificate, framed in black and hanging on the wall. She went to the University of Vermont. On the other wall are three pictures of the human body, one showing the skeleton, one showing the muscles, and one showing the organs. Everything is labeled with Latin words. It's hard to believe all those things are packed inside me. All of us walking around with our stomachs nestled under our rib cages and our intestines coiled up like sausages.

"Brendan, please cooperate with me." Dr. Phillips raises her voice to get my attention. "Mrs. Clancy is really worried about you. You won't talk to her. She thought you might talk to me."

I turn my attention to a chart showing the parts of your ear. So many parts, so many chances for something to go wrong.

"I'm really tired and I ache all over," I tell her. "Can I go home now?"

Dr. Phillips sighs and leads me back to the waiting room. Mrs. Clancy is reading a *House Beautiful* magazine, but she looks up hopefully. I sense Dr. Phillips shaking her head — *No, he didn't tell me a thing.*

Mrs. Clancy stops at CVS to get my prescription for Cipro filled. I shiver in the air conditioning. It's because I have a fever, Mrs. Clancy tells me. Soon I'll feel better.

In the afternoon, I fall asleep and dream about my mother. She comes to me dressed in clothes the color of summer leaves, gold and deep green, shot through with splashes of yellow like sunlight. She wears a wreath of wildflowers in her hair—bachelor's buttons, Queen Anne's lace, black-eyed Susans, and others I don't know the names of. She tells me she must return to the forest and she's taking me with her. We'll live in a tree there. Just before I wake up, she leans close to my ear and whispers, "I'm the daughter of the Green Man. I would have come for you sooner, but I've been under a spell."

It's like a story I used to tell myself when I was little. I had lots of stories then. Sometimes my mother's a Gypsy who travels with a carnival. She's a sword swallower, she eats fire, she walks on tightropes and dances on stilts, she paints her face white and her lips red. She puts dots of red on her cheeks. She draws eyebrows like the wings of birds. She wears clothes sewn together from snips of this and that. In every town she comes to, she looks for a boy who might be her long-lost son. When she finally finds him, she takes him with her and teaches him to juggle and walk tightropes and dance on stilts.

When he's older, she'll teach him to swallow swords and eat fire.

There's a sad story too. In this one, my mother is lost. She wanders down dark roads and through moonlit woods. She's searching for the baby she left behind because she had no way to take care of him, but she doesn't know how to find me or where to look. I'm a question at midnight, a few words whispered by the wind, a blurred reflection in rippling water, a voice in falling rain. My mother's hair is long and dark and her face is pale and sorrowful. She weeps in the shadows. She has no place to go, no one to love. I cry if I think about this story too long.

But no more stories. The truth is, my mother isn't looking for me. She has five kids and she wishes she'd left them all at the hospital. Their noses run, their clothes are stained, she wishes she could run away from them and her husband. But she never does because she can't think of a place to go.

But this is a story too. Maybe it's closer to the truth than the other stories, but it's still a story. Something I made up when I was eight years old.

With a sigh, I roll over and watch the leaf shadows shift and change on my wall.

I spend a few days in bed. At first I'm too tired to do

anything but stare out the window. Somewhere out of sight is my tree and my tree house. I picture the platform I built so carefully and the one below it that Shea and I built together. I wonder where the Green Man is and what he's doing. Part of me wants to see him but another part is still angry and disappointed.

Mrs. Clancy is obviously frustrated. She misses a day of work. She brings me meals in bed. She gives me medicine every six hours, which means she has to get up at night. There's a lot of sighing and muttering. She keeps asking me who beat me up, who cut my hair.

She goes on and on about the Green Man, whom she continues to refer to as the town drunk. Or one of them. He isn't the only bum she's seen drinking in the park. It's not wise to hang out with a man like him, she says—he might, he could have, he didn't, did he?

No, I tell her, he didn't.

"Well, I've sent him packing," she says. "He won't show his face around my house again."

"He came here?" I ask her. "To see me?"

She purses her lips and gives me the pouty look I hate. "He asked how you were. I told him I didn't want him near you, I know who he is, I've seen him in the park with the others. I said I'd call the police if he bothered you. He left soon enough, I can tell you."

I turn my face to the wall. He might not be the Green Man, he might have lied and pretended to be something he wasn't, but Mrs. Clancy shouldn't have chased him away.

"You want some ginger ale?" Mrs. Clancy asks.

I shake my head. She doesn't understand. She never will.

On Monday, the doorbell rings. I hear Shea say, "Mr. Hailey asked me to bring Brendan his homework so he won't get behind."

"Thanks. I'll tell him you were here."

"Can I come in and see him? Please?"

"Just a minute." Mrs. Clancy walks down the hall and opens my door. I'm pulling on my jeans, so she looks the other way.

"That girl's here," she says, "the one I saw at Mr. Hailey's house. Can't tell if she's white or black or something in between. You want to see her?"

"Of course I do. Her name's Shea and she's my best friend." I push past Mrs. Clancy.

Shea stands at the front door, her face pressed flat against the screen, waiting for me.

"Don't tire him out," Mrs. Clancy tells Shea. "He's been very sick." *And I've had to take care of him and miss work, which I can't afford, and it hasn't been a pleasure, I can tell you.* Of course she doesn't say this, but I know she's thinking it.

Shea and I sit in the lawn chairs on the porch. "Guess who I saw on the way home from summer school?" she asks. "The Green Man. He was waiting on the corner near the school. He wants to know how you are and when you're coming back to the tree house. He says Mrs. Clancy won't let him near you."

"It's true," I say. "Mrs. Clancy hates him. You'd think he was the one who beat me up."

"She can't stop you from seeing him. What's she going to do — follow you everywhere? I can just see her trampling through the woods, grumbling and muttering."

We both laugh. We imagine Mrs. Clancy in disguise — wearing sunglasses, a blond wig, a trench coat, trailing us like a bear heading for a blackberry bush. *Crash, snap, rustle, crash,* here she comes.

"He told me his real name," Shea goes on. "It's Edward Calhoun, but he says we can call him Ed."

Ed, I think. *Ed.* How can I call him an ordinary name like Ed? It doesn't suit him. "Do I have to call him Ed?"

Shea shrugs. "I don't care what you call him as long as you know he isn't the real Green Man."

I fold my math paper into a square. "He isn't the Green Man, but . . ." I don't know how to finish my sentence, so I just let it stop.

Shea looks thoughtful. "In a way, he *is* the green man," she says. "But without the magic. He told me he's lived in the woods ever since he came back from Vietnam. He has a sort of tent made of a camouflage tarp and log walls. When you get well, he says he'll show it to us."

"I feel pretty good now." I fold my math paper smaller and smaller, creasing the folds with my thumbnail, and then I toss it at her.

Shea ducks, grabs it, and throws it at me. We bat it back and forth, back and forth. It bounces all over the porch with Shea and me in pursuit. We make so much noise, we don't hear Mrs. Clancy until she says, "What are you doing? Do you want to have a relapse, Brendan?"

Shea looks like she's ready to run for home, but I grab her arm to stop her. "Can Shea and I go for a walk?" I ask. "I feel great. Honest."

"He looks great," Shea tells Mrs. Clancy. "Except for his hair."

We both laugh and Shea adds, "If anyone asks, he can say he got scalped by the worst barber in town."

I rub my head. The scabs are still there and they itch, but at least they don't hurt. Mrs. Clancy did her best to trim the tufts Sean left. My bruises are yellow and green instead of red and purple and black, but my ribs still hurt from being kicked.

"All right, all right," Mrs. Clancy says. "Go for a walk but don't be gone long. You haven't got your strength back, Brendan. A few blocks, that's all."

Truthfully, I'm glad she says that. My legs feel weak and wobbly from lying in bed so long. I don't think I can make it to the woods.

Shea looks at me as if she expects me to argue, but I shrug and say, "Okay."

We're halfway down the front walk when Mrs. Clancy calls, "And another thing—if you see that man, don't talk to him."

Shea looks at me. "Does she mean Ed?"

"Of course." *The pervert, the drunk, the bum,* I hear Mrs. Clancy say.

"Why does she hate him so much? Does she think he'll molest you or something?"

"She has a small mind." I measure with my fingers about an inch apart.

"Like most adults," she says glumly. "They always think the worst."

"Maybe we should run away to Never Never Land," I say.

"To do that, we have to trap Peter Pan's shadow in a bureau drawer. And then, when he comes to get it, he'll teach us to fly and then . . ." She stops and frowns. "And then and then and then."

"And then we grow up. But we stay just like we are now. Inside, I mean. We will never be real-lifers — the kind of people who think big expensive houses and fancy clothes and boring jobs are all that matters."

We crook our little fingers together as a promise and head down Main Street. Shea has enough money for sodas, so we stop at Joe's Diner and grab seats at the counter. The waitress looks at me. "What happened to your hair?"

"He had brain surgery," Shea says in a low voice. "They had to shave his head and saw his skull open and take out a tumor the size of a grapefruit. If you think he looks bad now, you should've seen him last month."

The waitress flushes and looks away from me. "I'm so sorry," she murmurs, and busies herself fixing sodas.

Shea and I start laughing. We try to stifle it but we can't. The waitress comes back with our drinks. "If that's your idea of a joke, it's not funny," she tells Shea, and slams our glasses down on the counter. "That will be three dollars. I was going to give him his for nothing, but not now."

Shea shoves three wrinkled dollar bills across the counter and the waitress takes them. The cash register is at the other end of the counter. She rings up the sale and stays there without looking at us again.

It's three thirty, too late for lunch and too early for dinner, so the diner is almost empty. Two old ladies are sitting in a booth having coffee and talking loudly about their grandchildren and how ungrateful they are because they never write thank-you notes. "I'm not giving Emily a birthday present next year," one says, and the other agrees. "Shannon won't get one either."

"Those cranky old ladies are definitely real-lifers," I tell Shea.

"And so is the waitress." We glance at her. She frowns at us. We are not funny. We are not cute. We are not nice.

We finish our sodas and trade the fresh cold air of the diner for the hot stale air outside. It smells like it's been breathed and rebreathed by thousands of people — used air, you could call it. No longer fresh.

Even though I'm really tired, we walk through the town park, a place I rarely go for fear of meeting one of my enemies. The benches are occupied by old people, some dozing, some just sitting. They remind me of passengers at the rail of a boat, waiting to see land. The swings hang on their chains, empty except for one little kid who is pumping as hard as he can. He looks like he's hoping to fly over the top and launch himself into outer space. At the base of a Confederate soldier's statue, I see Sean and his friends. Three teenage girls have stopped to talk to them. The girls fiddle with their hair, shift their weight from hip to hip, giggle.

I grab Shea's arm and pull her away, turn back to the park's entrance. She looks at the boys. "It's them, isn't it?" she asks. "The ones who beat you up."

"Yes." I walk faster, fearful of hearing one call out, *There he is.*

Shea hurries after me. "I know who they are. They live around the corner from me in those apartments at the end of the street. They sell drugs. The cops are always after them."

When we're a safe distance from the park, I sit down on a bus stop bench to catch my breath. Shea sits next to me.

"Do you think Sean is a real-lifer?" Shea asks.

I think about it, not sure what to say. "He's something else. He wants what real-lifers have, though—money, cars, houses, vacations, all that stuff. But . . ." I shrug and lift Shea's arm to look at her watch. "It's almost time for dinner. Mrs. Clancy's going to be furious."

We walk together to the end of my street. "Will you be in summer school tomorrow?" Shea asks.

I nod. We say goodbye, and I walk slowly up the street. In this neighborhood, the houses are one-story ramblers made of brick, probably all built at the same time because they seem to come in three basic look-alike styles. One has the front door in the middle. One has the front door on the left. One has the front door on the right. All have at least one picture window. Some have shutters, some have fences, some have lawn decorations. American flags flutter from most of them.

All of them are as tidy and well cared for as Mrs. Clancy's house. They remind me of an old Beatles song about Penny Lane and blue suburban skies.

Several men push loud power mowers up and down their lawns. Someone cooks hamburgers on a grill. The smell sometimes tempts me to become a carnivore. A woman waters her flowers.

Except for the lawn mowers, it's a quiet summer evening. Long shadows make the grass look even greener.

I realize I don't know a single person on this street. No kids my age live here. Maybe that's why.

FIFTEEN

MRS. CLANCY LOOKS UP from the pot she's stirring and frowns. "Well, look what the cat dragged in. I thought I told you not to be gone long."

I slide into my seat and watch her ladle pasta and sauce on my plate. "Marinara," she says. "No meat."

I watch steam curl up from the pasta. It's way too hot for a meal like this, but I figure I'd better eat it since she went to the trouble of leaving meat out.

She sits down across from me. "You know what? I talked to that pediatrician about growing boys needing meat, and she said not to worry about it, just to make sure you get your protein from cheese and nuts and things like that." She waves a hand at the shaker of Parmesan cheese. "Take as much as you like."

I sprinkle a pile of grated cheese on the marinara sauce and watch it melt. Mrs. Clancy does the same.

"You know something else?" she asks. "Dr. Phillips said it's good for people my age to cut back on red meat. She gave me a pamphlet about cholesterol and suggested I talk to my doctor about it."

This might be the most Mrs. Clancy has ever said at dinner. Usually she eats with one eye on the little TV she keeps on the kitchen counter, but tonight it's turned off. I wonder what else she's told Dr. Phillips about me. And what Dr. Phillips has said she should do with me, the problem boy.

Suddenly she stares across the table at me, a frown creasing her forehead. "I've been thinking about that girl. Is she really the only friend you have?"

The question takes me by surprise. To avoid answering, I swirl my spaghetti around my fork. It's finally cool enough to eat.

"Pretty much." I sop up sauce with my bread.

"Is one of her parents black?"

"Well, her mother's white and her stepfather's white, but all I know about her real father is that he was killed in Afghanistan." I look her in the eye. "Why do you want to know? What difference does it make?"

Mrs. Clancy takes a sip of iced tea. "I just wondered, that's all."

She *just wondered. That's all.* Mrs. Clancy doesn't need to know anything about Shea. Or me. It's none of her business.

"It's too late in the summer for Little League," she says, veering off in a totally different direction, "but soccer season's coming up. Maybe in the fall, when school starts . . ."

She breaks off with a sigh. "Dr. Phillips says I need to accept you just the way you are, but if you, if we — Oh, I don't know what to do with you. It's not as easy as she thinks."

For once she isn't angry. She doesn't raise her voice. She doesn't spout the usual stuff — I'm irresponsible, selfish, lazy, etc., etc., etc. She actually sounds like she's trying to start over with me. But she doesn't know how. Well, I don't know how to start over with her.

Mrs. Clancy sits there for a moment tearing her bread apart, not eating it, just crumbling it. "I've been taking care of foster kids for twenty years and never had the problems I've had with you." She frowns. "Don't get me wrong, Brendan. I'm not saying it's all your fault. I just don't have the energy I once had. I ought to be more patient with you, I know I should, but I don't have the patience I once had either."

I don't know what to say, so I start clearing the table. I watch her get up. She moves slower than she used to, and there's a white stripe along the part in her red hair. Her hands are ropy with veins. It's true. She's getting old. I surprise myself by asking if she wants some help with the dishes.

"That would be nice." Mrs. Clancy washes and I dry. We don't talk, just stand side by side as if we've been doing the dishes together for years. Outside the window above the sink, I can see the man next door working in his garden.

"You want to watch TV?" she asks. "*Jeopardy!*'s on after the evening news."

This is something new. She's never invited me to watch TV with her. Cautiously I join her on the sofa, leaving lots of space between us. I don't feel comfortable, but I think it might be smart to keep on her good side — which I honestly didn't realize she had.

The local weatherman is talking about the heat wave, which will continue all week. Temperature in the upper nineties, humidity to match, air quality is bad, and old people should stay inside. So should people with asthma.

Mrs. Clancy says, "Thank the lord for air conditioning. When I was your age we didn't have anything but window fans. We spent a lot of time in cool places like movie theaters and drugstores."

"The people I stayed with before I came here didn't have air conditioning," I tell her. "It was horrible."

The weatherman concludes by mentioning a hurricane is gathering strength off the coast of Cuba. Charlotte could pack a wallop if she hits the East Coast but there's nothing to worry about yet.

"It won't come this far inland," Mrs. Clancy says. "Heavy rain, maybe. Some wind. That'll be the worst of it."

She leans forward. The *Jeopardy!* music has begun. Alex Trebek walks out smiling and greets the audience. "Isn't he the handsomest man?" she asks. "I've been watching this show a long time and he just gets better-looking every year. I wish I knew his secret."

"Rich people always know stuff we don't," I say.

The contestants join Alex and he starts the introductions. One is a schoolteacher from Missouri, another is a lawyer, and the third is an accountant. All three are men. The accountant has won for three weeks in a row and he has twenty thousand so far.

Mrs. Clancy sighs. "I wish I was smart enough to get on the show and be a bigtime winner."

"What would you do with the money?"

"First I'd quit my job at the card shop and go on a cruise. I might even try my luck at one of the casinos in Atlantic City. You can take a bus from Roanoke."

The game starts before Mrs. Clancy has a chance to lose her winnings in Atlantic City. I wonder if she'd take me on the cruise — probably not. Probably I wouldn't want to go anyway.

The first contestant picks the category English Literature, and I amaze Mrs. Clancy by giving all the right answers. At the end of the show, she stares at me. "For somebody who almost flunked sixth grade, you sure know a lot," she says. "Why, with a brain like yours, you could win millions on *Jeopardy!*"

We watch a few more shows, but by nine o'clock I'm ready for bed. The new Mrs. Clancy has tired me out. I don't know how long our détente will last, but I have a strange feeling we might get along better now. Except for her questions about Shea, she was really nice tonight. Dr. Phillips must have given her an earful.

The next day, I go to summer school. As soon as we're dismissed, Shea and I cross the train tracks and head for the woods. Soon, the trees close in around us. Their straight trunks tower above us, soaring like pillars in a cathedral. We breathe in the smell of damp earth and moss. Above our heads, leaves rustle and sigh. Sunlight flashes down here and there in shafts the color of pure gold and puddles the ground with light. A bird sings *bloggit, bloggit, bloggit* over and over again.

As usual we walk quietly, Shea and I. We don't talk above a whisper. She knows the law of the forest.

We scramble up the tree and check our stuff. It seems like we've been gone for a long time, but everything is just the way we left it, except for a few acorns squirrels have dropped.

Suddenly the bushes part below us and the Green Man steps into the clearing. He's wearing a T-shirt with Bob Dylan's picture on the front and a list of concerts on the back with dates from 1988 to 2000. It was black once, but now it's faded to a greenish color. If he'd been wearing that shirt the day I met him, I wouldn't have thought he was the Green Man.

It's the first time I've seen him since he carried me to Mr. Hailey's house, and I'm not sure how I feel about him. Part of me is still mad, I guess. But there he is, old and shabby, grinning at Shea and me like we're still the best of friends. I don't know. Maybe we are. Maybe we aren't.

Shea calls down to him, "Hey, you got a new T-shirt!"

He smiles. "My other shirt disintegrated. I got this for twenty-five cents at the Goodwill store." He scratches his belly. "Dylan and me go back a long way."

He squints up at us, shading his eyes with his hand. "Come on down here. I want to get a good look at you, Master Brendan. I've missed you, lad."

"I've missed you, too," I admit. I scramble down the tree with Shea just behind, showering my head with rotten wood and bark.

The Green Man studies me. "Your hair's growing back," he says. "Pretty soon you'll look like those boring real boys with crewcuts. You're still skinny, though."

"He'll always be skinny." Shea gives me a poke in the ribs, which makes me wince. "Oops, sorry, I forgot about your bruises."

Shea and I share our lunch with the Green Man. Which is fine, because Shea brought more than enough for the two of us. Maybe she knew who'd be here, hungry and thirsty.

After we finish eating, the Green Man stretches out on his back and stares up at the treetops far above our heads. "I love the way the sun shines through the leaves," he says, "and how the trunks all seem to curve in and form a roof."

He looks like he might fall asleep, but Shea has other

ideas. "You promised to show us your hut," she reminds him. "Can we go there now? Please? Please?"

"You sure you want to see it?" The Green Man scratches his belly. "It's a hidey-hole, not very clean, a bit dark and damp and full of junk."

"Yes," she and I say. "Yes."

With a shrug of his heavy shoulders, the Green Man shambles ahead like a big bear. We follow him a long way into the woods, on a trail so faint and twisting, it might have been made by a deer — or a unicorn that didn't want to lead anyone to its hiding place.

He stops near a tall, twisted tree almost as old as my tree. Moss furs its bark with a thick green coat. "We're close," he says. "You can almost reach out and touch it from here."

Shea and I peer this way and that. We brush bushes and branches aside, ducking brambles, avoiding poison ivy. We look up in case it's a tree house. We look down in case it's truly a hole in the ground.

"It's not here." Shea's lower lip juts out like it does when she's mad.

I stare at him. Not so long ago, I would've thought he'd cast a spell of invisibility on his shelter.

"Come." The Green Man leads us off the path and

down a hill, threading his way between lichen-splashed boulders that erupted from the earth thousands of years ago. You can still feel the power that thrust them aboveground, only it's dormant now.

We're in a ravine beside a creek before we see the hut. Like Shea told me, it's a combination of canvas tarps and logs and cinder blocks. The canvas has a camouflage pattern. Grape vines and blackberry bushes cover it. The logs and cinder blocks are covered with moss and lichens.

"You have to be less than six inches away to figure out what it is." I keep my voice low. Who knows who could be listening or watching from the dense shade?

"And even then you could miss it," Shea whispers. "It's like a fairy's cottage, hidden from everybody, unless the fairy allows you to see it."

She looks at me, and I see a glint in her eye that tells me she's thinking maybe he's the Green Man after all.

The Green Man walks around to the side facing the stream and moves a pile of branches that hide a small door, as gray and weathered as the old logs on the ground.

"Come in." He steps back, and we duck our heads to go through the doorway. He bends down and comes in behind us.

As my eyes get used to the dark, I see a mattress and

blankets, an orange-crate table and an old office chair. Bits and pieces of metal sheets keep out the rain and snow.

In the light of a kerosene lantern, Shea examines everything, including the contents of an old wooden box. She rummages around and holds something up. "Are these yours?" she asks the Green Man.

He glances at what she's found — army medals on faded ribbons. "Ah, put those back where you found them."

"Did you get them in Vietnam?" she asks. "Were you a hero?"

"Me a hero, that's a laugh. Put them away, Shea. That box is private."

"This one's a Purple Heart," she says, "and this one's a Bronze Star. You want to know how I know?"

"Well, I suppose you'll tell me whether I say yes or no."

I'm watching all this anxiously. Is he mad at Shea? Is he about to kick us out? But he doesn't seem cross. Just resigned. Like me, he knows Shea pretty well now. She won't stop asking questions until she hears what she wants to hear.

"Well," she says, "my real father was killed in Afghanistan and the army sent my mother a letter about how brave he was and she has two medals just like these—a Purple Heart because he was wounded in battle and a Bronze Star because he was very brave."

Shea turns the medal over and reads the back: "'For heroic or meritorious achievement.' And here's your name: Edward John Calhoun. And here's a *V*, which means you got this for doing something brave in battle, just like my daddy. He saved two men in a burning tank and then got shot. I think he should've gotten the Congressional Medal of Honor for that. I mean, how much braver can a person be?"

"Not much," says the Green Man.

"What did you do to get yours?"

"Oh, Shea, can't we talk about something else?"

"Please tell me."

"It was so long ago, another lifetime. I barely remember the war. Or what I did. Or how I survived."

"Come on, Shea," I say. "If he doesn't want to talk about it, it's okay. Just leave him alone."

"Well, if I got a medal I'd want everybody to know why I got it and how brave I was." She holds one up to her chest. "And I'd wear them every single day. I'd never hide them away in a box."

"Everybody's not like you," I say.

Shea puts the medals back in the box and closes the lid. "Okay," she says, "but promise to tell me later."

"Maybe," the Green Man says.

"No maybes!"

"All right, all right. Someday I'll tell you all about it."

"Is that a promise?"

"Yes, yes it is." He's beginning to look a little vexed. "Now leave it be." He laughs when he says this, but I worry that deep down he's sorry he brought us here.

"Can I ask one more question if it's about something different?" Shea asks.

The Green Man winks at me. "Ask away, my dear."

"Do you sleep here every night?"

"If you go to the same place often enough, someone's bound to follow you. I sleep on a park bench in town when the weather's good. Sometimes I go to a shelter. Sometimes I spend the night under the bridge on Forty-Second Street. When it rains, I come here. And in the winter."

He points at a rusty potbelly stove in the corner. "I rigged up a chimney for that, but I only use it when it's really cold. Somebody might notice the smoke if I light it too often."

"Do you have enemies?" Shea asks.

I don't say anything, but I know he has three enemies, the same three I have.

The Green Man shrugs. "Well, for one thing, this is a national forest. People aren't allowed to live in it. The police would be delighted to dig me out of here and send me elsewhere."

He pauses and glances at me. "And then there's the three louts who think my comrades and me are fair game."

"What do you mean?" Shea asks. "What do they do?"

"Ah, they jeer at us in the park, throw stones at us, threaten us. After dark, of course, when no one's around to see them."

"Sean," Shea guesses. "And Gene and T.J. That's who you're talking about."

He nods. "The same brutes that beat Brendan."

"They wouldn't hurt *you*, though." Shea chews on her thumbnail and frowns. "Not like they hurt Brendan."

He glances at me, a warning to keep my mouth shut. "No, no, Shea, of course not. I might be old, but I'm as smart as a fox. Like a true Green Man, I can slip into the trees and disappear. Don't you worry about me."

Shea leans over and hugs the Green Man. "If I had a grandfather," she whispers, "he'd be just like you."

"Good lord, I hope not — a grandfather living in the

woods and drinking with his comrades in the park?" He laughs and then coughs, deep and rumbly.

"Maybe you could be our *adopted* grandfather," Shea suggests. "You'd like that, wouldn't you, Brendan?"

"I've always wanted a grandfather," I say.

"So will you please please please be our grandfather?" Shea asks. "Say yes!"

"Do I have to go to court and sign papers?" he asks, looking worried.

"No," I say. "It's just between us."

"Well, then I'll be pleased and honored to be your adopted grandfather." He shakes our hands solemnly. "Now I'll take you back to your tree house. It's almost suppertime."

We walk silently down the trail, which was made by deer, the Green Man says. At the tree house, he hugs us both. "This is a very happy day for me," he tells us. "I gave up hope of being a grandfather many years ago."

We watch him disappear into the shadows darkening the woods. He makes no noise. He leaves no trace of himself. Magic still clings to him.

Shea and I stand together silently. The trees tower over us. They were here before we were born, and they'll be here after we're gone, living their secret life, still and watchful.

"He's so mysterious," Shea says in a low voice, almost as if she's afraid to say it out loud. "There's so much we don't know about him. Like who he was before he went to war. Where he lived. If he has a family."

I'd never thought of the Green Man as having an ordinary life—I guess because I'd believed he was the true spirit of the forest, an ancient being whose existence went back to almost the beginning of the world.

"I think he likes being our adopted grandfather," Shea says.

"I'm glad you asked him. I'd never have had the nerve. I'm always scared people will say no, so I don't ask."

Shea shakes her head. "You're so silly, Brendan. You just have to take a chance sometimes." She spins around on her toes like a ballerina, then darts ahead of me through the trees. If I didn't know better, I'd think she was an elf queen vanishing into the twilight.

"Wait!" I run after her. She laughs, but she doesn't let me catch her until we reach the train tracks.

SIXTEEN

ALTHOUGH SHEA AND I GO to the woods after school every day, we don't see the Green Man. We spend hours looking for his hideaway, but we can't find it even though we're sure we're on the right path.

On the way back, Shea says, "It's as if he magicked it away."

I swat at the mosquitoes humming around my ears. Without my hair, it must be easier for them to get at my skin. "Let's go to the park. Maybe he's there."

Shea nods. "And if he's not, maybe his comrades can tell us where he is."

It's a long hot walk from the woods to the park, but Shea has babysitting money in her pocket and she promises to treat me to a soda. But not at the diner. We don't want to see that waitress again.

None of the Green Man's comrades are there. In fact, the park's deserted. Near the fountain, we see bright yellow tape circling an area. Two police cars with flashing blue lights are parked on the path.

"What do you think happened?" I ask Shea.

"Probably somebody snatched a purse or something."

We watch the cops for a while, but they aren't doing anything more exciting than standing around and talking in low voices. We go on to McDonald's and get our sodas to go. The air conditioning gives me goose bumps. Shea shivers.

The next day, Mr. Hailey tells Shea and me he wants to talk to us after class. Shea gives me an *Uh-oh, what did we do?* look, and I shrug. Can't be anything too bad. We're both passing everything.

After the other kids leave, Mr. Hailey sits on the edge of his desk. His face is serious. "I'm really sorry to tell you this," he says, "but Edward Calhoun, your Green Man, is in the hospital. He was attacked in the town park and badly beaten."

Shea's face turns pale. Tears run down her cheeks. One leg jiggles like she's lost control of it.

I sit there like a lump. Paralyzed or something. If I

open my mouth, no sound will come out. It's not true, not true, not true.

"Is he going to die?" Shea's fists clench.

"My wife checked on him. He's in stable condition — that's better than critical condition."

"That's what the yellow tape was," Shea whispers. "That's why the police were there. And we didn't know, we didn't know! We had no idea it was for him."

"How could you know?" Mr. Hailey says.

"I should have known," she says. "I should have felt something."

Shea is sobbing now, and Mr. Hailey is trying to comfort her. I stand and watch the two of them. I feel cut off. Alone. Why don't I cry? What's wrong with me? Numb, that's what I am. Like my whole body just got a shot of Novocain.

"Has he said who did it?" I ask Mr. Hailey.

"According to today's paper, Mr. Calhoun was unconscious when the police found him. When he came to, he said he couldn't remember. It was dark, they jumped him from behind."

"Cowards!" Shea wipes her eyes with her fists and says, "I hate them, I hate them. First they beat up Brendan, and now the Green Man."

Mr. Hailey looks puzzled. "What are you saying, Shea?"

"Sean Barnes and his friends. They jumped Brendan on the train tracks, and the Green Man said they bug him all the time. Jeer at him. Make fun of him. Threaten him." She takes a breath. "Who else could it have been?"

"It might have been anyone, Shea. You mustn't leap to conclusions. You have no evidence Sean Barnes is behind this. I know he's a mean kid, but —"

"But? But?" Shea turns to me. "Tell him, Brendan. You know it was them."

I don't look at her or Mr. Hailey. Why didn't I let Mrs. Clancy call the police? Why didn't I tell them who beat me? If I had, maybe this wouldn't have happened. Maybe it's all my fault the Green Man is in the hospital. I stare at the gray linoleum floor, too ashamed to speak.

"Brendan." Mr. Hailey bends slightly to look me in the eye. "It's not your fault. Even if you'd given the police Sean's name, they wouldn't have had much of a case. No one saw them beat you up. They would have denied it. Your word against theirs. Without a witness, I doubt they would have been charged with anything."

I stare at him. He's read my mind as if my head is transparent.

"Come on," he says. "I'll drive you home and come back at six thirty to take you to see him. If it's okay with your parents, that is."

Without another word, we follow Mr. Hailey to his car. Shea gets in the front seat. I get in the back. He takes me home first because I live closer.

Mrs. Clancy is watering her flowers. She stares at the car as if she's expecting bad news. *He's cutting school again, he's not doing his homework, he's failing summer school.*

Shea waits in the car, but Mr. Hailey crosses the lawn to talk to Mrs. Clancy. He tells her about the Green Man. She knows already. She read it in the paper this morning, but she didn't tell me.

"Since the man means a lot to Brendan, I'd like to take him and Shea to the hospital after dinner this evening. If that's all right with you."

"No, it's not all right," Mrs. Clancy says. She's gripping the hose as if Mr. Hailey might yank it away from her. "I told Brendan he's to have no contact with that bum."

"He's not a bum," I say. "He fought in Vietnam and he has two medals, the Purple Heart and the Bronze Star for bravery."

"Lots of men in this town have been in a war," Mrs. Clancy says. "They don't live in the woods, they don't sit in the park and drink. They raise families and go to work and live a regular, normal kind of life."

She doesn't get it. Some people can't live in the world she's talking about. They aren't comfortable there, they don't believe in jobs and houses and cars. They can't do what you have to do to get them, and if they try, they make themselves miserable. It's like a train when it switches to another track and goes full throttle down the main line but there's this rusty little spur line that curves off into the woods. Only a few people ride the train that goes down those tracks.

"He's a good person," I tell her. "He's hurt, he's in the hospital. You have to let me see him."

Behind me, I hear Shea say, "Please let him go, Mrs. Clancy. Please."

"Brendan's right," Mr. Hailey says. "Mr. Calhoun is a good man. I wouldn't take the children to see him if I thought otherwise."

Mrs. Clancy knows when she's defeated. She shrugs and says, "All right, all right. He can go."

"I'll pick him up at six thirty," Mr. Hailey says.

Mrs. Clancy turns her attention to the garden. She's

not happy about the situation and she doesn't want to talk about it. I wave to Shea and Mr. Hailey and start to go inside, but Mrs. Clancy stops me.

"Give me a hand with the weeding," she says.

At six thirty, Mr. Hailey pulls into the driveway. Shea sits beside him. We look at each other but we don't say anything. We're both scared, I think, of seeing the Green Man in the hospital.

Shea's wearing a denim skirt and a pink T-shirt with a big butterfly on the front, an outfit I've never seen before. She looks different, older or something. She must think visiting the hospital is a dressy occasion. Maybe it is. I climb in the back seat and hope my jeans are okay.

It begins to rain. Taillights shine on the wet road, and the traffic lights blur red, green, and yellow. No one talks. We sit and listen to the music on the radio. It's an oldies station. I recognize Bob Dylan singing "Don't Think Twice, It's All Right," which reminds me of the Green Man's T-shirt and the years when he was young and a soldier in Vietnam.

Mr. Hailey parks in the hospital lot. We dash through puddles. The sliding glass doors open as if we're expected. People hurry inside with dripping umbrellas. Some carry flowers. Others carry balloons with smiley faces. A departing woman says to her husband, "He doesn't look good." "He looks better than I expected," her husband says, and unfurls his umbrella with a snap.

After we get visitors' passes at the front desk, Mr. Hailey leads us down the hall to the elevators. While we're waiting, a nurse comes along. She must be Mrs. Hailey's friend, because she stops to say hello to Mr. Hailey.

"What brings you here on a night like this?" she asks. "Your wife's shift doesn't start till eleven."

Mr. Hailey puts his hands on our shoulders. "Brendan and Shea have come to see Ed Calhoun."

The nurse looks puzzled. "I didn't expect him —"

Mr. Hailey must have given the nurse a look Shea and I couldn't see, because she stops in midsentence and says, "I hope you find him feeling better."

After the nurse walks away, Shea looks at Mr. Hailey. "What didn't she expect?"

"I haven't the foggiest idea."

She probably didn't expect him to have any visitors, I think.

The elevator doors open silently and we get in quietly. Nobody says anything. On the fourth floor, the doors slide open and we step off, still saying nothing.

We walk down a long hall, past trash cans labeled

HAZARDOUS WASTE, a cart stacked with dirty plates, a wheelchair or two draped with blankets, a couple of gurneys, and medical equipment on rolling stands. It smells like medicine and something undefinable. It's as if the normal air has been used up and we're breathing something else. Fake air, maybe. Every once in a while someone pages a doctor or calls for a nurse. Things buzz and beep.

People cough. TVs flicker, but there's no sound. Nurses pop in and out of rooms. Through an open door, we see bare feet sticking out of the bedcovers. "Gross," Shea whispers.

A man comes along hunched over his walker, trailing an IV stand. He's wearing a skimpy little hospital gown that doesn't quite cover his skinny backside.

"Gross," Shea whispers again.

I don't answer. I keep my head down so I won't see anything. I wish I had earplugs and a nose clip so I wouldn't hear or smell anything.

The hospital is the scariest place I've ever been, worse than a haunted house, worse than a graveyard. I want to run outside into the rain and dark before someone decides I have to stay here.

At last, Mr. Hailey stops at Room 412B. Edward Calhoun's name is on a card under the number. Shea grabs my hand. Hers is small and warm, and I'm afraid to hold it too tightly.

I stare at the man in the bed, his eyes closed, lying so still, connected to tubes and blinking, beeping machines. His beard is gone. His head is bandaged. One arm is in a cast. His fingernails are clean. He doesn't look like himself. Maybe we're in the wrong room.

"What did they do to him?" Even though Shea whispers, I can tell she's angry, partly because she's squeezing my hand so hard it hurts and partly because she has that dangerous look on her face.

Mr. Hailey shakes his head. "He was badly beaten, Shea. On top of that, he has pneumonia."

Shea releases my hand and tiptoes to the Green Man's side. "Are you awake?" she whispers.

His eyelids flutter and open. "Lady Shea, my little princess of the woodland."

His eyes find me and he beckons me closer. "And here's Sir Brendan."

I look into his eyes, as blue and clear as ever, and I know it's truly him. "I hope you feel better soon." It's such a stupid thing to say. So trite. I might as well have told him to have a good day. But my mind is numb, and I can't come up with anything else.

"Will you come home soon?" Shea asks.

The Green Man gazes into space as if he sees something beyond the walls of the room. "Ah, yes," he says, "I'm on my way home now. Should be there before dark."

His voice turns into a cough, a deep, horrible chest-wrenching cough that leaves him gasping for air. Mr. Hailey bends over him. "Lie back and rest, Ed."

"Don't worry," the Green Man says. "I'll soon have all the rest I need."

His eyes begin to close. His chest rattles with every breath as if something inside is choking him.

Mr. Hailey takes Shea's and my hands. "We should leave now," he says softly.

The Green Man opens his eyes. "Thanks for coming," he tells us.

"I love you, Grandfather," Shea whispers, and kisses his pale cheek.

He touches her curls and smiles. "Love you too, little maid."

He turns to me and takes my hand. "Brendan, my lad."

There's so much I want to say, but his eyes are closing and his grip on my hand loosens.

Neither Shea nor I want to leave, but a nurse arrives and says we must go. As Mr. Hailey leads us toward the door, Shea and I look back at the Green Man, lying in his pure white hospital bed, surrounded by machines. His eyes are closed, but he raises one hand in farewell.

In the corridor, Shea begins to cry. "He's not going to get well, is he?"

"No," Mr. Hailey says softly. "He probably won't make it through tonight."

Shea grabs my hand again, and we walk slowly away from Room 412B. My head is a jumble of thoughts and fears and sorrow. I can't find a way to express how I feel. I can't cry, either. It's over. The Green Man is leaving, he's going home, and the forest will never be the same. Nothing will.

SEVENTEEN

W HEN WE LEAVE THE HOSPITAL, the rain pours down. Even though it's only seven thirty, it's almost dark. The road is practically deserted. In Price Chopper's parking lot, streetlights shine on scattered shopping carts. Every now and then the wind gusts and sets them rolling across the asphalt. The traffic lights sway.

"It's the hurricane," Mr. Hailey says. "It swung inland off the North Carolina coast. We're in for a lot of rain and wind."

When Mr. Hailey drops me off at my house, I see Mrs. Clancy at the door. The living room glows with warm light. Buffeted by the wind, I run though the rain and dash inside, wet already.

"Get your pajamas on," Mrs. Clancy says, "and we'll have a cup of hot chocolate."

We sit together at the kitchen table. The rain sluices down the windows, hiding the darkness outside.

"He's dying," I whisper.

"I'm sorry to hear that," Mrs. Clancy says.

"He's a good man," I tell her.

Mrs. Clancy sips her hot chocolate. She doesn't look at me or say anything. Outside the wind rises and the rain falls harder. I look at the window and see our reflection in the glass. This is how we'd look to a stranger. A woman and a boy sitting in a cozy kitchen, drinking hot chocolate.

After I go to bed, I sense the Green Man's presence in my room, sitting in the shadows, watching over me. I'm afraid he's died and his ghost has come to say goodbye. I burrow under the covers and press my face into my pillow.

"Please don't die," I whisper to him. "Please, please, please."

When I wake up, it's so dark I can't believe it's morning. The sky is black and rain batters the house, the yard, the garden. Trees whip back and forth in the wind, blurred as if I'm looking at them underwater. The side yard is flooded ankle-deep, and branches litter the grass.

"No power," Mrs. Clancy tells me. "They don't know when it will be restored. Lots of trees are down."

We eat cold cereal. Mrs. Clancy can't fix coffee. She drinks a soda instead but complains that it doesn't have nearly as much caffeine as coffee. After breakfast, we stand at the back door and watch the rain come down. It pours over the eaves like a waterfall. The wind puffs the screen door inward. I smell rust and wet grass and water and mud.

"My poor flowers," Mrs. Clancy says. "Just look at them. The rain has flattened them."

I wander back to my room and pick up *Riddley Walker*, a book Mr. Hailey thought I'd like. It takes place way in the future after nuclear bombs practically end the world. Even though the words are sometimes hard to understand, I like the book a lot, probably because I'm always expecting "the one big one" to destroy civilization.

The phone rings and I jump, startled by the sound. "Lucky we have a landline," Mrs. Clancy says as she goes to answer it.

She speaks in a low voice and then calls me. "It's Mr. Hailey. He has something to tell you."

From the way she says it, I know what he's going to tell me. I don't want to hear it. I stare at the receiver as if it's dangerous. Mrs. Clancy moves it closer, her face sad. Slowly I lift it to my ear.

"I'm so sorry to tell you this, Brendan," Mr. Hailey says, "but Ed Calhoun died in his sleep early this morning. My wife was with him. She says it was very peaceful. He just slipped away."

I hold the phone so tightly it hurts. My old beliefs about him rise in my mind. "He's the spirit of the forest, the Green Man," I say. "He can't be dead. Not him."

I hear Mr. Hailey say, "He was a man like everyone else, Brendan. Mortal." His voice is calm. Accepting.

I shake my head. Mrs. Clancy puts her arm around me.

"Are you okay?" Mr. Hailey asks.

"Yes," I say. "Thank you for telling me." Very quietly, I lay the receiver in its cradle. I am not okay. My legs shake. Something is gone from the world. Something is missing.

Mrs. Clancy hugs me. "I'm sorry, Brendan."

I stand stiffly, not used to being this close to her. She smells of soap and perfume. I try to hug her, but I can't. I stand next to her with my arms at my sides and her arms around me.

When she releases me, I step back. "He died in his sleep," I say.

"He was old and sick, Brendan." She pauses. "Sometimes people are glad to go."

I don't answer, but I know I'll *never* be glad to go.

The phone rings again. This time it's Shea weeping into the receiver. "We'll never see him again," she sobs.

What can I say, what I can tell her? It's true. We'll never see him again. No one will. The Green Man is gone. This time he won't return.

I go to my room and lie down. The rain falls, the wind blows. I read, I sleep, I eat a cheese sandwich and an apple for lunch, but I'm not really hungry. I go over every moment I shared with the Green Man. I wish I hadn't gotten mad at him for pretending to be what I wanted him to be. I wish I hadn't torn up my drawings of him. But he understood. I know he did. And he liked being our adopted grandfather, even though it was for such a short time.

That night, Mrs. Clancy and I eat a cold supper by candlelight and use flashlights to find our way around the dark house.

A couple of days after the hurricane ends, the power comes back. Mr. Hailey and his wife arrange a funeral and burial for the Green Man. It will be a graveside service, he tells Shea and me. As far as anyone knows, the Green Man didn't go to church and most likely wouldn't want a Christian burial.

No, I think, of course he didn't. Green Men are pagans. Maybe I'm a pagan too.

Mr. Hailey drives Shea and me to Ivy Hill Cemetery. He parks behind a hearse on the downward slope of a small hill. The rain has stopped and the sun is shining. The sky is the color of the Green Man's eyes.

Shea's hand creeps into mine. Her fingers are small and cold. But strong. They grip my hand tightly.

Three men from the park are already there, standing together under a tree. Their clothes are old and faded like the Green Man's. They have beards and shaggy hair. One wears a straw hat and another has a baseball cap with his hair sticking out in a gray ponytail. Their faces are worn and rough and sad. They nod to us but they don't come closer. They keep their distance and watch.

The only other people there are two gravediggers waiting to finish their job. One has tattoos on every visible part of his body — Celtic designs, serpents, and stuff. I wonder how much it hurt to turn himself into a work of art.

A coffin sits above an open grave. Shea tightens her

grip on my hand. She turns her head aside. If she doesn't look at the coffin maybe it won't be there, and the Green Man will join us, laughing at his big joke.

Mr. Hailey says a few words and his wife lays wildflowers on the coffin lid.

"Would anyone else like to say anything?" Mr. Hailey asks.

The man wearing the baseball cap steps forward. "You were a good man, Ed," he says in a hoarse voice. "We'll miss you, buddy. What happened to you shouldn't have happened to a dog. Rest easy, nothing can hurt you now."

He steps back and the other two nod. "You said it for us, George," one says.

The other says, "That was a man won't come our way again. We was lucky to know him."

Still clinging to my hand, Shea whispers, "Rest in peace, Grandfather."

I say the words I memorized this morning:

> Fear no more the heat of the sun
> Nor the furious Winter's rages,
> Thou thy worldly task hast done,
> Home art gone, and ta'en thy wages.

I speak in a low voice, just for the Green Man to hear. I feel him all around me. In the breeze, in the sunlight, in the fresh smell of the grass, in the sky above and the earth below. He'll always be with me, no matter how long I live.

"He won't be out in the cold anymore," Shea whispers. "He won't be hot and sweaty. Or get wet in the rain. Or be hungry. He's gone home."

The gravediggers slowly lower the coffin into the dark hole. The Green Man's friends join us to drop a handful of dirt on the coffin.

"Dust to dust," Mr. Hailey says, "and ashes to ashes."

We stand back and stare down at the shiny coffin spattered now with handfuls of dirt. Shea presses her face against Mrs. Hailey's blouse and cries. I look up through green leaves to the sky and feel the warmth of the sun on my face. "Fear no more," I whisper, "fear no more."

The man in the baseball cap pats my shoulder. "That was a nice thing you said. Ed loved poetry, recited it all the time."

He smiles at Shea and me. "You must be Brendan and Shea. Ed sure was proud of you two, always saying how smart you were and what good kids you were. You gave that man something to be happy about, which is a damn fine thing."

He pauses and gestures toward the men under the tree. "That's Charlie and Joe over there. They're shy about meeting people. I'm George." He holds out his hand and I shake it and so does Shea.

George and his quiet friends wave goodbye. We watch them walk across the cemetery until they're lost from sight among the tombstones.

"Come on, you two," Mr. Hailey calls. "It looks like it's about to rain again. Let's get you home."

Before we get into the car, Shea and I look back at the Green Man's resting place. The gravediggers have filled in the hole with a backhoe and are hard at work laying sod over the red earth. We both hate to leave him there. Especially with rain on the way.

By the time Mr. Hailey stops the car in Mrs. Clancy's driveway, the sun has slipped behind the clouds. You can smell rain coming.

"I'll meet you in the woods," Shea whispers as I get out of the car. "We need to make sure the tree house is safe."

"Okay." I wade through puddles in the driveway but I don't go inside. I know I should change my clothes and tell Mrs. Clancy about the funeral, but I don't want to talk to her. In fact, I don't want to talk to anyone, not even Shea. I need to be alone in my tree house so I can think about the Green Man.

I cut through the side yard, hoping Mrs. Clancy won't see me, but as I skid down the muddy hill to the train tracks, I think I hear her calling me. At the bottom, I run across the tracks and into the woods.

The ground is soggy, and wet weeds brush my legs, soaking my shoes and pant legs. The air is hot and thick with humidity. It smells of dampness and decay. It hums with gnats and mosquitoes. Tree branches and leaves litter the ground. I see fallen trees leaning on each other like pickup sticks. Mushrooms have sprouted everywhere, some in circles, some poking up from the storm's rubbish. A breeze shakes drops of water from the trees onto my head.

At least the rain seems to be holding off. The sky is purple dark, though, with big clouds. It's coming, I think.

As I near the clearing, I notice an empty place in the sky. "No," I whisper. "No."

I run through wet bushes and brambles and burst into the clearing. What can't have happened has happened. The tree is down. Its roots tower above my head.

Its massive trunk has taken smaller trees down with it. Its branches are still green with leaves.

I'm witnessing a tragedy. The tree was a king, almost a god, the real Green Man of the forest. It must have lived through hundreds of storms. And now it's a dead giant sprawled on the ground, Achilles in his armor dead on the battlefield.

I don't know what to do. The place where I belong is gone. The Green Man is gone.

While I stand there staring at the tree, the rain begins. Soon it's beating down through the branches and pounding my head and shoulders.

I run into the woods, tripping and stumbling. Wet branches slap my face and brambles snatch at my legs. Crows caw in the branches over my head.

I slow down. A voice in the back of my mind asks me why I didn't wait for Shea. *She's your friend, your only friend,* it says. I have no answer. I want to be alone, that's all.

Am I going the right way? All the trees look the same. So do the rocks and boulders, hills and valleys. For all I know I've been running in circles. People do that when they're lost. But I'm not lost. That boulder over there — I remember it because it looks like the Green Man's profile.

I go on slowly, not sure I'm right until I hear the stream, rushing over stones, almost hidden by trees. I follow it, scanning the bushes carefully, and finally I see it.

I look behind me, but no one's there. Cold and wet, I slip through the trees and crawl into the Green Man's shelter. I know he's not here, but his spirit fills the place.

I lie down on his bed, which is as damp as everything else. Why does everything change? Why can't he be here? Why did he have to die?

I hear Mr. Hailey say, *He was a man like everyone else. Mortal.*

Mortal, I think. *Mortality.* That's what *mortal* means even though you don't think of it every time you hear the word. We are all mortal. We will all die. Even the Green Man. Even me.

No, I think, *no. Not me. Not Shea.* I want to run, like someone in a story trying to escape fate. Gilgamesh, maybe. But you can't escape. You can't run far enough, you can't hide. No matter which direction you go, death is always there, waiting for you.

I lie still and breathe in the smell of mildew and decay. Rain drips through the roof. I notice that the Green Man put out buckets to catch it.

The shelter grows darker. The rain falls harder. I know it's late. Mrs. Clancy will be mad—no, I correct myself, she'll be upset I'm not there, but she'll act mad.

Silence rings in my ears. I'm alone. Like always. Brendan Doyle, boy freak.

Suddenly there's a noise in the bushes. Shea crouches in the doorway, drenched with rain, her hair a black tangle of drooping curls. She's been crying. And it's my fault.

"Why didn't you wait for me?" she asks. "I went to the tree and it was lying on the ground, and everything we had is smashed and ruined. I waited there. I thought you'd come and maybe I could make you feel better, we could make each other feel better, but you didn't come and you didn't come and then I knew you didn't wait for me." She stops and takes a breath and wipes her nose.

I try to think of an excuse, but she starts talking before I can say a word.

"I've been wandering around the woods for hours. I thought this is where you'd be, but I couldn't remember how to get here. And I thought I was lost and I'd never find my way home and I was cold and I was wet and I was scared."

By now, she's standing next to me, shivering with cold. "I'm sorry," I tell her. "I just wanted to be alone."

She wipes her eyes with the back of her fists like a little kid. "Do you want me to go away?"

"No. Not now. I'm glad you're here."

She smiles a wobbly smile and sits down in the Green Man's sagging office chair. "No wonder he got sick," she says. "It's so damp and cold in here." She shivers and rubs her arms to warm herself.

"What will we do without him and our tree?" I ask.

Shea looks down at her wet running shoes and sniffs. "I don't know," she says in such a sad, low voice that I can barely hear her.

We sit together and watch raindrops plink into the buckets. What is there to say?

I sigh. "I guess we should go home."

"Should we take his box with us?" Shea asks. "I think he'd want us to."

"If we don't," I say, "someone might find this place and wreck everything."

She removes the box from its hiding place and hands it to me. "If I bring this home, Cody and Tessa will get into it. Nothing's safe from them. I can't even keep a diary."

Together we leave the shelter and fasten the door as best we can. I cradle the wooden box in my arms, close to my chest, trying to shield it from the rain.

Shea and I walk through the woods silently. I think, *This is how it is when you're with a friend*. You don't need to talk all the time. You can just be together and think your own thoughts.

EIGHTEEN

I SNEAK INTO THE HOUSE. Women's voices float through the kitchen from the living room, which means Mrs. Clancy is too absorbed in the TV to notice I'm soaking wet as usual. Or even to hear me come in.

I tiptoe to my room and close the door softly. After yanking off my wet clothes, I stuff them into the back of the closet and pull on jeans and a T-shirt. Hopefully I can add my slacks and shirt to the next load of laundry without her noticing.

Sitting cross-legged on my bed, I open the box. The medals are on top where Shea left them. I lay the Bronze Star and the Purple Heart reverently on my pillow and run my finger over the cold metal. The Green Man received these when he was young. When his whole life lay ahead of him. Before he went to live in the woods. Before he grew a bushy beard.

The medals waver as if they're underwater, and I realize I have tears in my eyes. I wipe them away. I never cry. Never. But the tears fill my eyes again and I lie down, press my face into the pillow, and let myself cry for the Green Man and the tree and my mother — yes, my mother, who will never come back for me. I cry for her, too, the unknowable, the stranger I could pass in the street and not recognize.

When my tears finally stop, I blow my nose and look through the other stuff in the box. I find three of my drawings of the Green Man and a carving I made of him. I almost cry again.

I pick up a handful of foreign coins — Vietnamese, I guess. His expired driver's license from 1981. His discharge papers, his birth certificate, and his high school diploma are in the box, rolled up, damp, stuck together, too mildewed for me to read more than a few words here and there.

I put everything back, close the lid, and shove it under my bed. Then I open my door, ready to face the wrath of Clancy.

When I appear in the living room, Mrs. Clancy jumps and almost drops her coffee. "Brendan," she cries, "you nearly gave me a heart attack! How long have you been home?"

"You were watching TV, so I went to my room and I guess I fell asleep." I yawn in what I hope is a convincing way.

"You should have poked your head in and let me know you were here."

"I didn't want to disturb you."

"The funeral couldn't have lasted all that time," Mrs. Clancy says. "Where did you go afterward?"

I shrug. "Shea and I got sodas and we talked about the Green Man and then we went to her house for a while and her mother gave us lunch . . ." I let my voice trail off into an embarrassed silence. I really don't like lying to her, but she's never known about the tree house and how much time I've spent in the woods.

"What is this about the green man?" Mrs. Clancy asks. "Why do you keep calling poor old Mr. Calhoun that?"

"Well," I say, "I call him the Green Man because he's . . . he's — well, he just is."

"What are you talking about?" Mrs. Clancy shakes

her head. "The only green men I ever heard of are Martians. Aliens flying around in spaceships. Surely you don't believe that old man came from outer space?"

"No, of course not. The Green Man is the ancient spirit of the woods. He protects the trees and the forest creatures. And Mr. Calhoun, well, he's like him, that's all." The expression on her face makes me stammer to a stop.

"Excuse my ignorance, Brendan, but you've lost me. Why would you think Mr. Calhoun is like an ancient spirit?"

"It's hard to explain." Now I'm embarrassed. Why did I think she'd understand? "He knows the forest. He can tell you the names of trees and birds and plants. He can even identify a bird by its song. And he moves through the trees without making a sound. You know how all of a sudden deer are there and then they're gone and if you weren't looking, you wouldn't know they were there? That's how he is."

Mrs. Clancy nods as if she's trying to figure this out. "Well, it sounds pretty far-fetched to me. It must be all those books you read and that imagination of yours. Me, all I see is what's real." She tapped the coffee table. "Solid. Nothing mystical about it. Just a table."

She heaves herself up and heads for the kitchen. "Time to think about dinner."

The next morning, I set out for summer school. Mrs. Clancy doesn't drive me there any longer. She trusts me. It's almost over now anyway. No reason not to finish and go on to middle school with Shea.

I cut through the park. A little out of the way, but it's early and I have plenty of time. Near the fountain, I see George, Charlie, and Joe huddled together on a bench. Sean, Gene, and T.J. are flicking lit matches at them and laughing.

"We looked for you last night, but you weren't here," T.J. says to them. "Scared you might get beat up like your buddy?" He makes a fist as if he plans to hit George.

"You ought to be locked up for what you did to Ed," he says in a low voice.

"Nobody saw us but you," Sean says, "and who's going to believe an old drunk?"

"Nobody cares what happens to bums like you." Gene leans over George, his face inches away, almost nose-to-nose with him. "Your breath stinks like cheap wine."

While this is going on, Charlie and Joe shrink into themselves. They don't say a word in George's defense. They don't look at Sean. They sit there like scarecrows.

A cop walks toward us. Before he notices anything, Sean and his friends saunter away, laughing.

"Okay, boys, move on," the cop tells the men on the bench. "I've told you before not to loiter in the park. You give the place a bad name."

My heart pounds, but I step out of the shade and say, "Officer, those guys, the ones who just walked away, they were threatening these men."

The cop stares at me. "I didn't see them do anything."

I come closer. I run my hand over the stubble on my head. "The same guys beat me really badly a few weeks ago." My voice shakes and my knees tremble. "They cut my hair off with a knife. I had cuts and bruises all over me. You can still see the scabs."

"Why didn't you report it?"

"They said I'd be sorry if I told anyone." I glance at the men on the bench. All three are watching the cop and me. "They beat Mr. Calhoun to death."

The cop frowns and stares hard at me. "Wait a minute. Do you know that for a fact?"

"Ask George," I say. "He saw the whole thing."

George gets up, ready to run. "Oh, now, Brendan, don't drag me into this. I didn't see anything."

The cop turns from me to George and grabs his arm to keep him from disappearing into the park. "Ed was your pal," he says. "If you know something about his death, you owe it to him to tell me."

"They'll kill me, too," George mutters.

The cop scowls. "Not if they're in jail."

So instead of going to summer school, I go to the police station with George, Charlie, and Joe. The cop turns us over to a team of detectives. Detective Gifford takes me to his office and calls Mrs. Clancy.

I cringe when he tells her he has me in the station and he needs her presence because I'm a juvenile. "No, Brendan's not in trouble," he says. "He's here to report a beating." A pause. "No, no, not another one. He's finally ready to identify the boys who attacked him."

While we wait for Mrs. Clancy, Detective Gifford treats me to a soda and asks me the usual questions about myself. Favorite subject in school—art. Favorite sport—none. He raises his eyebrows slightly. "What do you do when you're not in school?" Read, draw. He asks what my favorite book is. I tell him *The Lord of the Rings*. He's read that, so we talk about Middle-earth and hobbits and elves and wizards and magic. We discuss the movies and agree Gollum was amazingly well done, all pretty true to the book, and wouldn't it be great to go to New Zealand and see where the movies were filmed.

Just as we're about to exhaust the subject, Mrs.

Clancy walks in, dressed for the occasion in her best slacks and a pale blue blouse.

"Why aren't you in school?" is the first thing she says. "This is the last week, Brendan. Don't let me down now."

For a minute, I think the old Mrs. Clancy is back and she's going to tell the detective what a lazy, unreliable, irresponsible boy I am.

"I cut through the park and the guys who beat me were harassing Mr. Calhoun's friends and then a cop came along and I told him those guys — Sean and Gene and T.J. — beat me up and cut off my hair and I was pretty sure they beat Mr. Calhoun, too."

Mrs. Clancy sits down. She clasps her big, shiny purse as if it's a life preserver. "Brendan was badly beaten," she tells Mr. Gifford, "but he never told me who did it. He said he didn't know their names, they were strangers. He thought they didn't like his hair or something. It was long then, past his shoulders, and I wanted him to get it cut, but oh, no, he wouldn't go to the barber. Kids teased him about it all the time."

She pauses, out of breath, I think. "He's a good boy," she adds. "Not a mean bone in his body. But he doesn't have any sense and he's stubborn as all get-out."

I slide down in my chair. A good boy, I think. She's never said *that* before. I steal a look at her and she actually smiles.

"Tell the detective exactly what happened," she prompts me. "I want those monsters put in jail for what they did to you. And to that poor old man."

So while Mrs. Clancy listens, I tell Detective Gifford I saw T.J. running away from the jewelry store in the mall the night it was robbed, and T.J. thought I told the police. He and his friends cut my hair off and beat me black and blue.

"Then Sean held a knife to my throat and said if I told anyone about what happened, I'd be sorry. The Green Man — Mr. Calhoun, I mean — told me they roughed him up when he tried to stop them from shooting squirrels, and George can tell you they beat Mr. Calhoun the night he was taken to the hospital."

Leaning back in his chair, Detective Gifford looks at me, his face troubled. "I wish you'd reported this right away."

"He wouldn't even tell *me*," Mrs. Clancy puts in.

"I was scared."

Detective Gifford rubs his chin. "Yes, I know. I understand that." He goes through some papers on his desk. "The boys have a record," he says. "Theft, robbery, break-ins, drugs, simple assault. Unfortunately, we can't use any of that against them when they go to court."

"Why in the world not?" Mrs. Clancy is outraged. "The jury needs to know what kind of boys they're dealing with."

Detective Gifford spreads his hands as if to say he understands but he can't do anything about it. "They've been charged and punished for their past offenses. Knowing their record would prejudice the jury."

Mrs. Clancy shakes her head. "No wonder we have so many criminals walking the streets."

"Don't worry," Detective Gifford tells her. "We have enough here to put them away for a while — simple assault, aggravated assault."

Mrs. Clancy leans toward the detective and asks, "Are you going to put out an all-points bulletin to pick them up?"

Detective Gifford smiles as if he knows Mrs. Clancy watches cop shows on TV. "It's already been done."

I write a statement and sign it. Mrs. Clancy gives her consent for me to press charges against Sean, Gene, and T.J. Then we're free to go.

Outside in the blinding summer sunlight, Mrs. Clancy says, "I wish you hadn't missed school to do this, but it's good you finally reported it." She opens the car door and lets out a wave of trapped heat.

"I'll never understand why the jury shouldn't be prejudiced," she says to herself as she starts the engine and turns on the air conditioner. "Those boys should be sent to jail for life."

———

NINETEEN

At THE END OF THE WEEK, we have a little ceremony. Most of us receive certificates to go on to the seventh grade at Long View Middle School. All the parents clap hard, but Mrs. Clancy claps the hardest.

Mr. Hailey takes me aside and gives me his personal congratulations. "See what you can do when you try, Brendan? Straight A's. Promise me you'll keep this up in middle school."

He holds out his hand and I shake it. "I wish you could always be my teacher."

"Maybe I will be," he says. "I teach math at Long View, you know."

"That's great." I wave goodbye and join Shea at the refreshment table.

"The punch is pukey," she warns me. "But the cupcakes are delicious, especially the chocolate ones."

Since she has chocolate all over her mouth, I figure she's sampled a few already.

While we eat, Shea and I talk about what middle school will be like.

"We won't have just one teacher," she tells me. "We'll have someone different for each subject."

That's good, I think. I won't be stuck all day every day with someone like Mrs. Funkhauser.

"And we'll change classrooms," Shea goes on.

"How do you know all this?"

"Carmel told me."

"Who's Carmel?"

"She lives in the apartments across the street from me. She's in the eighth grade, but you'd think she was in high school. She's got boobs bigger than her head and she wears tons of makeup, but she's actually very nice. Not too smart, though."

When I don't say anything, Shea adds, "And you know what? If anybody tries to pick on me, she'll beat them up. She's promised to be my bodyguard."

I wonder if she'll be my bodyguard too, but I'm ashamed to admit I might need one.

"Do you think you and I will be in the same homeroom?" I ask.

"I hope so." She chews on her thumbnail and looks me over. "Your hair's growing back. Are you going to keep it short or let it grow?"

"Mrs. Clancy wants to take me to the barber for a trim before school starts, but I'm letting it grow. It's my hair and I like it long."

Shea grins. "You and me — nobody tells *us* what to do. Carmel says I should wear makeup, at least lipstick, and get a padded bra, but I'm not doing either. My mother's on Carmel's side but my stepfather's totally against it." She laughs. "I never thought *he'd* be on my side."

It embarrasses me to think about Shea wearing a bra, so I don't say anything. I'm glad she's not going to start using lipstick and girly stuff.

Mrs. Clancy comes over to tell me it's time to leave. Shea wipes her mouth with a napkin and says hello.

Mrs. Clancy actually smiles at her. "Congratulations on passing summer school," she says. "Did you know Brendan got straight A's?"

She grins and nods. "I did too. We're the stars of our class."

"Well, isn't that nice. I hope both of you get straight A's in middle school."

"Don't worry," Shea says, "we will. Right, Brendan?"

I shove my hands in my pockets and say, "Maybe."

Mrs. Clancy cuffs me lightly on the shoulder. "Don't be so modest, Brendan."

The next day, Shea and I go down to the woods to start our search for the perfect tree to build a new tree house. We pass the grove where our tree lies on the ground. The sun is hot for September, especially with no tree to shade us. Wildflowers have grown up around the stump, and butterflies and bees flit from one blossom to the next, never staying long in one place.

"We'll never find another tree like this," Shea says. "It must have been a thousand years old. Maybe more."

"Even if we did," I say, "it wouldn't be the same."

We walk along the trunk from its huge root ball until we lose our way in a forest of small branches. Shea pats a place for me to sit beside her. The trunk's so big that our feet dangle above the ground.

I catch sight of three deer moving slowly through

the trees, their backs dappled with sunlight. They stop and stare at Shea and me with big brown eyes, their ears erect.

"If you squint and make them blurry, they could be unicorns," Shea says.

"But they're not," I say.

Shea sighs. "Well, even if they are just deer, they're still beautiful and kind of magical. Don't you think so?"

I lean forward and study the deer. They stand so still, their heads up, their ears perked, their eyes focused on us as if they want to know who we are and if they can trust us. The trees encircle them and I feel the power of those trees. As silent and motionless as the deer, the trees watch us, too. If we make one wrong move, the deer will disappear into the woods without a sound. But the trees will stay where they are, held fast by their roots but vigilant.

I glance at Shea. Her eyes fixed on the three does, she's as still as the deer and the trees. Will she understand if I tell her about the trees and their magic? Or will she think I'm out of my mind?

While I hesitate, the deer walk slowly toward us, crossing the clearing step by step, never taking their eyes off us. Behind them, a breeze moves through the leaves, and I imagine I hear the Green Man's voice telling the deer we won't harm them.

The deer stop about two feet away, too far to touch them but close enough to see our reflections in their eyes. They smell like the woods, mossy and fresh. It's as if time has stopped and anything might happen. I realize I'm holding my breath and I let it out slowly. One deer lowers its head and makes a whuffing sort of sound.

In the softest voice I've ever heard, Shea whispers hello to the deer. The smallest of the three stretches its neck toward Shea and makes the whuffing sound again. If Shea raised her hand, she could touch the deer's soft nose, but she doesn't move. Neither do I.

Then, as if on signal, their white tails shoot up and they leap away. In an instant, they're gone, swallowed up by the woods.

Shea turns to me. "Do you think the Green Man sent them?"

I stare at the wall of green that hides the deer. "He might have. It's what he'd do if —"

We look at each other, still wanting to believe. The trees stir, the leaves whisper, a crow cries, its harsh voice filled with the dark wisdom of the forest. In my mind's eye, I see the Green Man at the edge of the woods. He raises a hand to wave, then vanishes into shadows.

In the distance, a train whistle blows. I slide off the tree trunk and Shea drops down beside me. Silently, we walk through the woods, toward home.

MARY DOWNING HAHN, a former children's librarian, is among today's best-loved authors of fiction for young readers. In addition to an Edgar Award and the Scott O'Dell Award for Historical Fiction, her books have won more than fifty child-voted state awards and have sold more than two million copies in all formats. *Where I Belong* is her thirty-first book. Mary lives in Columbia, Maryland. You can learn more about her at www.marydowninghahnbooks.com.